—— The ——
Ebony Cane

A Novel

Written by Carl Mendelsohn

FriesenPress

Suite 300 - 990 Fort St
Victoria, BC, Canada, V8V 3K2
www.friesenpress.com

Copyright © 2015 by Carl Mendelsohn
First Edition — 2015

All rights reserved.

Editor: Eva Almos

ISBN
978-1-4602-7777-5 (Hardcover)
978-1-4602-7778-2 (Paperback)
978-1-4602-7779-9 (eBook)

1. Fiction, Mystery & Detective

Distributed to the trade by The Ingram Book Company

ACKNOWLEDGEMENTS

FOR

Ruth, my wife, who inspired the character of Ruth,
Rose, my second wife, who encouraged me to complete the novel,
My children, Deena and Brian, who coerced me to complete the novel,
Luisa, who typed and corrected the manuscript,
Eva, my editor and agent, without whom I would still be in the wilderness

And

Erica, who shared with me her family's experiences in Hungary during
World War II and the subsequent occupation under Stalin.
With love and gratitude.

CHAPTER I

Winter was not yet over on this bright March day in 1950, and as if to let the world know that the seasons have their own humors, a steady snow kept falling, covering the roads and the lawns with a white powdery blanket. But it was a pleasant day, and not nearly as cold as it had been the previous week, and crocus bulbs appeared here and there, heralding in the beginning of spring. Calman Mencher emerged from the Imperial Bank of Commerce, just down the street from his office;which was located at Bathurst and Bloor Streets in Toronto. He looked again at the business card he held in his hand as he walked briskly towards his Vauxhall, settled in, and looked again at the card Dick Norris had given him. Two words greeted him – "Emeric Jewelry".

* * *

Dick Norris was young to be a bank manager, only thirty-one, and was just three years older than Calman. But he had worked for the bank for three years before enlisting in the army, and another six years since his return. Moreover, he was married and had already fathered three children, which was considered to be a sign of stability. And the fact that his father was also a bank manager didn't in the least hurt his chances for promotion in the banking establishment. Dick was thin, strong and wiry, and was a champion handball player. He and Calman had, in fact, met at the handball court at the YMCA gym. Dick waved Calman into his office.

"Is this the inner sanctum?" Calman asked jokingly.

"Actually, the inner sanctum is over there," Dick pointed to the basement, which contained the vault. He sat down in the swivel chair behind his desk and beckoned Calman to a seat facing him. "Would you care for a coffee, Cal?"

Calman glanced at his watch, "No, I'll pass thank you."

Dick opened the top drawer of his desk and withdrew a manila file folder containing a sheaf of papers. "The client's name is Stern, actually Shtern, recently arrived from Hungary," Dick said, scanning the papers.

"I wonder why he felt it necessary to change his name."

"Oh, a lot of immigrants do that. Besides, he's not really changing his name, just a minor alteration in the spelling. I would say that, symbolically, he is closing the book on the past, which was probably painful, and opening a new book. You know! A new name, a new country, a new life, and a new kind of hope."

"I suppose that by Anglicizing his name he hopes to become better integrated into this new world."

"Yes, and it's also good for business.

I understand," Dick continued, "that before the war they went by the name of Shternfeld. Anyways, perhaps I should tell you a little about the gentleman you are going to meet today. Emeric Stern is a man of about fifty and is the scion of one of the wealthiest Jewish families of prewar Hungary."

"Were they financiers or bankers?" asked Calman.

"In a way, you can say that because they had a lot of gold. They were actually in the jewelry business. They owned and operated the most prestigious jewelry house in Europe. Before the war, during the 1930s, they were represented in Germany, Austria, Poland and Czechoslovakia, and they were planning to open in Paris and London, but then Hitler came to power, and that brought an end to all their plans."

"Too bad!" Calman said thoughtfully.

"Yes!" Dick mused back: "The best laid plans of mice and men gang aft agley."

"Sounds like Robbie Burns," Calman conjectured.

"Probably!" Dick answered. He continued: "Now that they have immigrated to Canada they will be opening a jewelry emporium here in the heart of Toronto. They will need an accountant to help them set up their financial records, teach them about sales tax reports, employees' income tax deductions, etcetera. I recommended you highly."

He walked Calman to the door and handed him a card. "Thank you, Dick! I'm ever grateful to you."

CHAPTER II

As Calman headed south on Yonge Street in downtown Toronto, towards the new Stern business establishment, his mind turned to this new prospective client. What was this Stern person like, he wondered. The name, S-T-E-R-N, suggested to him a severe, rigid individual. He had some other European clients who were difficult… stubborn, contemptuous, inflexible martinets, who ruled, not just their businesses, but their families too, with an iron hand. He thought of the baron, another Hungarian émigré`, who dominated his wife and children, and who had rebuked Calman, *"Du bist der boochhalter."* This Emeric Stern was probably going to be difficult. "Yes," he thought, "I'm going to have to be authoritative with him. Otherwise he won't respect me…lose respect and you lose the client."

He now began to fantasize that once he had clinched this account his status as a public accountant would skyrocket, and he would then move his offices downtown to the financial district, away from his friend Charlie Tepper's law practice, next to the delicatessen. His own practice would start to grow as he attracted bigger and better clients, and of course, the bottom line of his personal income statement would take a meteoric rise. He crossed an icy patch on the road and the car began to swerve. That brought him out of his reverie.

"Well," he mused, "I've read up on the jewelry business, I've put on my best suit, I've had a haircut and a shave and dabbed on some cologne. I'm prepared for whatever happens." He pulled up on the east side of Yonge Street just south of Queen, and looked once more at the business card he held in his hand.

Calman looked through the car window for the entranceway to the emporium, but could not locate it. He backed up, thinking he had gone too far. Then he drove forward again, but he could not discern a jewelry store. He parked the car and again examined the card on which he had written down the address, and checked it against the addresses on the street.

All he could find was a nook recessed into the wall of a dilapidated store building. He looked into the store display window and saw a few antique relics of jewelry. The window itself was grimy and smudged. "Surely this is not the place," he muttered in disbelief, but there was no other jewelry store in the vicinity, and it was then that it occurred to him that the palatial business entity he had expected to find was nothing more than a small, penny-ante shop.

Disappointed, he locked the car door and started looking for the doorway. He found the door, which had a small card the same as Dick Norris had given him, tacked to it. The entrance to the shop showed the ravages of time. Peeled paint, cracked bricks, a broken stair informed the exterior of the building. He turned the door handle and the door gave way with a creak. The inside was just as ramshackle – unstuck wallpaper, warped floors, patched windows – but oddly, no dust. The floors had been swept clean and washed. Against the wall stood two glassed-in cabinets with shelves, "second-hand" written all over them.

Two antiquated showcases displaying their outmoded wares were located at the center of the room – jewelry of all kinds, mainly gold rings, pendants, bracelets, pins, necklaces, and an assortment of watches. This inventory was well suited to the surroundings—old, heavy, baroque, mid-European—belonging to a time long past. On one of the showcases someone had placed a thin ebony cane with a bone ferrule and an ivory handle. The handle had been sculpted into a fist clenched over a heart. Calman prided himself on being somewhat of a cane aficionado, and he boasted of a small collection of his own. He lifted the cane and ran his fingers admiringly over the smooth shaft, speculating that this would make a great addition to his collection.

As Calman was absorbing this drab, crypt-like chamber he suddenly felt a presence behind him, and quickly returned the cane to the showcase and turned around. A form had risen like a phantom from somewhere behind the display counter to greet him. He was the littlest and humblest man Calman had ever encountered —a gnome, barely five feet, four inches. He was bent, which not only accentuated his Lilliputian dimension, but also gave him an air of servility. He was clean-shaven, and his trim, dappled-gray hair, already sparse, was flat, combed straight back on his head. The wide forehead narrowed to a point at the chin. His black intelligent eyes were two craters, which, in combination with a thin aquiline nose protruding from the center of his hollow cheeks, gave him the appearance of a Halloween masque.

He was dressed impeccably in a dark gray suit and vest, a white shirt with starched collar and cuffs, and a black silk tie displaying a diamond pin. A gold chain extended across his vest from the left pocket to the right, which held a ponderous gold watch. This sartorial image was completed with a pair of exquisite platinum cufflinks and a thick gold ring, which burdened the middle finger of his left hand. This, Calman would discover, was his regular attire, which gave him the demeanor of an undertaker, or, at least of one in perpetual mourning. The gentleman proffered his hand.

"You must be Mr. Mencher, the accountant?" he enquired with some hesitation. Calman extended his arm smiling, and they clasped hands. They stood thus for several moments sizing each other up. Calman did not notice the door open, but suddenly he felt another presence in the room. A woman had entered, or rather, wafted into the room, quietly and innocuously, a pale smile lighting up her face, putting him in mind of a halo. Her hair, which was pulled back tightly into a bun, was prematurely gray. She wore a dark-colored tweed skirt with an ashy blouse, closed at the neck, and low-heeled brogues that made her seem mannish. But her dull attire could not extinguish her femininity. Within the folds of her skirt was the faintest suggestion of her sexuality—the thighs, the lush veld between the knees, the calves. Her two large brown eyes were set in an oval face. There emanated from her being a whisper of perfume.

Calman blushed as he felt an uncontrollable surge in his loins. But it was her bearing that most impressed him. In contrast to her husband's stoop, she carried herself erect, with stately elegance. Yet there was something sad, a taint of the tragic, about her appearance, Calman sensed, which made him recall a scene from the World War II movie, "Waterloo Bridge", in which the abandoned heroine, acted by Vivian Leigh, wanders desolately across the bridge. He estimated her age at fifty and conjectured that she had once been an exquisite beauty.

Stern introduced the lady: "This is my wife, Helena." She extended her reach towards Calman, and he took her hand in his and bent over it, as he had seen European gentlemen do. Her hands were very small—slight, and he noticed that her pellucid skin revealed the subtlest, bluish veins.

"Helen!" He thought of Marlowe's famous description of the Trojan princess—"Is this the face that launched the thousand ships?" Calman was a romantic, and he often caught himself lost in such reveries, making literary allusions. "My name is Cal," he said, addressing Mrs. Stern, "at least that's what my friends call me."

"Aha!" Mr. Stern enjoined, "Then it must be short for Calvin."

"No, my name is actually Calman. I inherited it from a great uncle whose name was in fact Kollman. My parents anglicized it by dropping the K and substituting a C."

"And my name is actually Helena," Mrs. Stern said, "but I dropped the 'a' when we came to Canada, and my husband dropped the 'h' at the end of his name." They chatted for a few minutes, and then Mrs. Stern excused herself and vacated the room, and Calman turned to her husband.

"You know," the gentleman explained, "our name is actually Shternfeld, but we were advised to shorten it, you understand, for business reasons only, when we came to Canada."

"And when did you immigrate to Canada Mr. Stern?"

"In September," he replied matter-of-factly.

"I see," Cal said knowingly, "so you've only been here six months." Calman caught himself. *He must think I'm a simpleton to draw such an obvious inference.* But he'd always had difficulty making small talk. Nodding towards the showcase he asked the proprietor, "Are these the goods you plan to sell here?"

"Yes," Stern acknowledged, "but I can get more."

The door opened again, and Mrs. Stern reentered the room carrying a tray on which rested a plate of strudel and two demitasse cups of espresso. Stern pulled up some chairs and the three of them sat down. "Please try this strudel, Mr. Mencher," Helen smiled.

"The name is Calman, but I would prefer you to call me Cal," he said, helping himself to a pastry. The strudel consisted of apple, nuts and Turkish Delight wrapped in a thinly, rarefied dough and baked to a brittle crisp. As Calman savored the taste he imagined that this must be what they eat in heaven. Calman now turned to the husband and wife. It was time to talk business. "When did you open this store?" he asked

"Last week," Stern replied.

"Have you signed a lease yet?"

"I have it here. I thought you might want to look at it before we sign."

"Good!" said Calman. "Now we have to speak candidly. Is that O.K. with you?" They nodded, and he continued: "I have two comments about your business, from what I have seen so far.

The first has to do with your merchandise. I see that you have a number of gold items and that you also carry some silver artifacts."

"Yes!" Stern interjected. "And we also sell gemstones".

"So I see. They must be very valuable. I hope you have insured your merchandise."

Stern looked at him quizzically. "Insured?"

"Yes! You have to protect them from loss due to theft, or fire, or any other risk. However, notwithstanding that, I think you will have problems marketing this merchandise."

"How would you know that?" asked the gentleman, as his wife listened intently.

"May I be blunt?" The couple nodded in unison. "I am not an expert in jewelry. Indeed my knowledge in your profession is very limited. But, it seems to me that your inventory consists of ponderous pieces... heavy and ornate. The jewelry that sells here is more like my ring," and he extended his ring hand for them to see, "light and stylish. That is the fashion."

Mrs. Stern looked at her husband and nodded as if to say, I told you so.

"And you said you had a second comment?" Mr. Stern interjected. He was paying close attention.

"Yes, my second comment pertains to your location. A retailer has to display his wares. You do not have a proper display window. You don't even have a sign, and people passing by don't know that this is a jewelry store. The store has to be appealing. You have to be prepared to spend a considerable sum to renovate the premises, both inside and outside so as make it presentable. So my advice is: 'Don't sign this lease, and don't remain here.'"

Stern looked from Helen to Calman and back, and announced relieved, "You are right on both points. You have saved us from making a big mistake." He opened a drawer and drew out a checkbook. "How much do we owe you Mr. Mencher?"

"Nothing," Calman replied, "the strudel more than made up for it."

Calman shook hands with Stern, and once more bowed over the lady's extended hand. Stern accompanied him to the door, and Calman then noticed that he walked with a slight limp. Calman gave him his business card, saying, "When you are ready to venture into business again please feel free to call me." He looked back at the charming woman and again there was a stirring in his loins. Embarrassed he immediately turned his attention back to the husband, "By the way Mr. Stern," he said, "I admire your walking stick. In fact, I collect canes as a hobby, and if you ever care to sell it, I would like to make you an offer."

"Thank you," he returned, "it belonged to my father."

CHAPTER III

The lease on the old tennis clubhouse ran out, and the landlord would not renew. A committee was appointed to meet with old man Winkler, but he was not to be persuaded to extend the lease. He was going to tear down the old firetrap and build apartments on the land. They were in great demand, and Winkler's decision made a lot of economic sense. September 30th was the final day. During the morning and afternoon the club championship finals were played, and in the evening the club threw a bash to celebrate the end of the season and the end of the club. Calman and his friend, Bennit Moranz, arrived, wearing short-sleeved shirts and slacks. They were met at the door by big Marty Sobelman, the wrestler.

"Hey guys, come on, you were told you have to wear jackets. You can't come in. Those are my orders." They could hear the mix of many voices and the music in the background.

"Marty do they have a live band?" Bennit asked.

"Yeah, they have Artie Shaw," he replied sarcastically. As the pair were about to turn around to go back to the car to retrieve their jackets, Calman caught a glimpse of a young woman whom he had not seen around before, and his heart stopped beating. Then she was gone.

"Come on," he said hurriedly to Bennitt, "let's get our jackets." The two Lotharios returned within a few minutes wearing jackets.

Marty smiled at them, "That's better," and waved them in.

Calman walked right into the club, his eyes scanning the room for the inamorata who had stopped his heart. Bennit stopped to joke with Marty.

"We almost came back without our pants, but my friend was in too much of a hurry to change."

"No objection," Marty quipped back at him, "it doesn't say anything in the rules about having to wear pants. It just says you have to wear jackets."

Bennit caught up to Calman, "You looking for someone special?"

"Yes, I thought I saw someone before we went back for our jackets, but now she seems to have disappeared," he dragged on his words in disappointment.

"What did she look like?" asked Bennit. But before Calman could answer him Bennit suddenly perked up: "Hey! There's Leslie…I'll see you later. I'm going over to ask her to dance."

Calman followed along leisurely, his eyes still searching the room. By the time he caught up to Bennit, Leslie was introducing him to a friend.

Leslie now turned to Calman, "Hello Cal, I would like you to meet my friend Ruth,"…but Calman's heart had started to miss beats again. Ruth extended her hand to Calman and gave him a glowing smile.

He did not release her hand. "Would you care to dance?" he asked and started to lead her onto the dance floor without waiting for a reply.

The dance was a slow number, giving him an opportunity to press her to him. He breathed in a subtle fragrance. He was ignorant about perfumes, but was desperate to make conversation. "Taboo?" he asked. It was the only name he knew.

"No," she laughed, "ordinary eau de cologne. I didn't think it was noticeable."

Ruth lived within walking distance from the club, and Calman walked her home that evening, leaving Bennit to escort Leslie. Usually Calman bantered with his dates or teased them playfully. Keep it light was his motto. But this evening Ruth drew him out, and the talk became serious. He realized soon enough that a skillful inquisitor was interrogating him, but he took pleasure in talking to Ruth about himself. At first they talked about his work, and then about his future plans. She listened patiently and with genuine interest.

"Leslie told me that Bennie is also an accountant. Are you partners?" she asked him.

"Oh, don't call him Bennie. He hates that name. Everybody calls him Benn or Bennitt. No, we are not partners," he said. "I like Benn, and we are good friends, but our personalities are too different. I'm afraid that if we were partners we'd have a falling out in the first week."

"Oh," she said surprised, "And how are you different?"

"Well, Benn is too pessimistic, and he lacks confidence in himself. He won't take risks." She looked at him quizzically. "Well, for example, he doesn't gamble, he won't play the markets, he won't even wager with me on the outcome of a tennis match, although he's the stronger player."

"I see! And what about you, are you a gambler?"

"No! Not exactly! But I will take a chance once in a while, you know, a calculated risk."

"I see," she mused, "What kind of calculated risk?"

"Well, we both started our practices about the same time. I borrowed a couple of thousand dollars to open an office. It was a wise move and paid off quickly. My practice has grown. Benn still works off the kitchen table in his parents' home. His practice has remained stagnant. Or, at least, so he complains to me."

"So, you are telling me that he is insecure, but you are not. Is that right? Don't you feel insecure?"

"Of course I do, but I don't let it cloud my judgment. I use my uncertainty to overcome my demons, whereas Benn allows his to undermine his confidence."

"I have to admit," she said, "that I am surprised because I found Bennit, or Benn, to be cheerful and clever this evening."

"Yes, that's why we're good friends." he explained. "Benn is charming in social situations and he can be quite witty, but when you get to know him better you realize that his wit is marked by a kind of cynicism, concealing a deep layer of self-doubt."

"I see," she murmured, "that's very discerning on your part." He was pleased with the compliment.

Ruth continued to query Cal, this time about his academic background. He bragged to her that he had an undergraduate degree in English and philosophy, and tried hard to impress her with his meager knowledge of Hegel and Schopenhauer. She plied him with questions, and he was only too glad to supply copious answers. But the more he thus expatiated the more incisive her questions became until he began to struggle with the answers. Soon he began to contradict himself and she sensed his discomfort. She ceased the inquisition, which he had brought upon himself, and he regretted his pretensions. They walked on, hand in hand, wordlessly, for a few minutes. Then he stopped abruptly and faced her.

"Say, it is my turn to ask a question," he said. "So tell me Ruth, what is your philosophy?" She took his hand again and they continued to walk.

After a short while, she said, "Emulate Socrates!" Little did Calman know that she had two master's degrees, one in sociology, the other in social work, with a minor in philosophy.

When they got to her home, they sat together on the old chaise on the balcony and schmoozed for an hour. Her mother came out on the pretext of bringing her a wrap because it was chilly. "After you leave she will cross-examine me on our relationship. Who *vas dem nayem boy*?" she parodied her mother. Ruth allowed Calman to kiss her. It was a lingering kiss, and she consented to see him the following evening. That night Calman could not sleep. An image of the brunette with the azure eyes, the high cheekbones and creamy skin, the ample breasts, the hourglass figure, and her patience with his effusive talk kept him awake all night.

CHAPTER IV

Calman had just finished showering, and was dressing for the evening, when the shrill ring of the phone startled him. "Damn," he muttered, "I'll have to mute that sound." He got to the receiver on the second ring. "Hello," he said, cocking the receiver to his ear as he began buttoning his shirt.

"Hello, Mr. Calman Mencher?" came a foreign voice.

"Yes, this is he," Calman replied impatiently.

"I don't know if you remember me, but here is Emeric Shtearn. You told me I should call you when I am ready." Calman sat down on the edge of the bed.

"Of course I remember you, Mr. Stern. It's been a while since we last met, almost a year I believe. How are you and Mrs. Stern? My mouth still waters when I think of your wife's strudel."

"Thank you, my wife will make more for you."

"So, Mr. Stern, do you still have those premises on Yonge Street?"

"No, I took your advice and gave them up."

"I see, so what are you doing now?"

"Well, I have designed a little jewelry in a more modern style, like you suggested, and have sold a few pieces."

"Well, that's good," said Calman, "and you've called at a propitious moment, because I'm getting married, and I need to buy both an engagement ring and a wedding ring."

"I will make something special for you. But the reason I called you is that my sister and her husband have arrived in Canada, and they want to go into business manufacturing syrups." Calman thought, *Syrups! That's unusual*, but he looked at his watch and saw that he was running late, so he merely retorted with "well I'd like to meet them."

"Mr. Mencher, that's why I called you. Could you come to my apartment tomorrow evening, say, around 8 o'clock?"

"That would be fine."

"And please, Mr. Mencher, bring your fiancée."

"Thank you! I will." He waited for the receiver to click at the other end before he hung up.

The elevator rose to the sixth floor carrying Calman and Ruth. At the end of the hallway they spied an open door to an apartment and two people standing in the doorway to greet them. Stern moved forward and shook hands warmly with Calman.

Calman introduced Ruth, "Mr. Stern, I would like you to meet my fiancée, Ruth. Ruth, this is Mr. Stern." Stern took Ruth's hand, bent over it, and brought it close to his lips, but fell short of actually planting a kiss on the hand. Calman observed the movement, and reflected, "So this is how the knights perform the ritual."

In the interval Mrs. Stern had remained stationary in the doorway. As the three of them approached the doorway Mrs. Stern extended both her hands towards Calman, her face beaming smiles of welcome, "It is so very good to see you again Calman."

"Cal," he interjected.

"All right, Cal." She turned to Ruth and embraced her: "We are delighted to meet you, Ruth," She gushed. "I am Helen."

Ruth replied with an infectious smile: "Cal has told me about you, Helen, and I am very happy to make your acquaintance too." There was an immediate rapport between the women, Calman noticed, as they walked into the living room, hand in hand. Stern went to a desk, beckoning Calman to follow him, and opened one of the side drawers. He withdrew a package containing several rings and called to Ruth,

"Would you like to see these, Ruth?" She came forward with Helen, and the foursome began examining the selection. Ruth selected a simple gold wedding band. Stern chose a similar ring with a single diamond setting.

"No," said Ruth, "I don't want anything ostentatious for a wedding ring. Just a simple band will do." They then selected a more elaborate engagement ring. "I'm afraid that will be too expensive," Ruth objected.

"Don't worry about the price," Stern said. "Calman and I will come to terms."

Calman now began to take in the room. He noticed that the ceilings were high, about ten feet from floor to ceiling. He thought to himself, *Our ceilings are no more than eight feet.* On each wall there hung a painting or a tapestry. Stern noticed Calman examining the wall hangings, and offered: "These tapestries come from Hungary. They were woven on a vertical loom. Notice how the threads are interlaced."

Calman had no knowledge about tapestries. But he ventured: "I see that they all depict religious scenes."

Ruth now joined the conversation: "I think they're medieval, some even mythical. Look! The fabric on the main wall has a unicorn."

Calman hadn't noticed the unicorn. Now he stood up and began to inspect the piece carefully.

"A fine piece of art," he commented.

Ruth quietly nudged Calman and whispered: "Take in the floors." They were of a stunning hardwood, narrow slats of oak. But it was difficult to see them because they were laden with Persian rugs, in some places two or three thick. Calman recalled the Persians he had seen in his grandparents' home. But they were thin and threadbare, and did not compare to those he was now discovering in the Stern residence. The rugs were plush and colorful, and Calman luxuriated standing on them.

Mr. Stern asked Ruth: "Do you like oriental rugs?"

"I simply love these," Ruth raved.

"Now don't get carried away with enthusiasm, Ruth. We can't afford the luxury yet."

"You can probably buy some very reasonably at any auction," Stern interposed. "Helen and I would be glad to go with you."

"What is this large rug at the bottom of this pile?" Ruth asked.

"Oh! It is a *farsh*, which simply means it is large. It is one hundred percent hand woven, and it comes from Tabriz in Azerbajdzan."

"I see! Is it an antique?"

"I would guess it is a hundred years old."

Calman now enquired: "What is this smaller rug on top of it?"

"Oh! That is a qalichep, a smaller rug. *It is actually a Kashan, and is made of silk.* And the smaller one you see here is a qum – silk on silk," Stern said very proudly

The conversation was cut short by a pounding at the door, and Mrs. Stern went to open it. "Tante, Tante," squealed a little girl as she ran towards Helen, followed by her younger brother, "look what I drawed for you." Helen lifted her up and curled her in her arms, hugging, kissing and fussing over her. Mr. Stern walked towards them smiling. Smiling was the extent of his emotional displays. The little fellow came towards him and wrapped his arms around Stern's leg. He would not relinquish the leg until his uncle bent down and patted his head. Their parents remained in the doorway treasuring the moment.

Helen addressed them, "Well, don't stand there like statues. Come in. Come in." And turning to Ruth and Cal, she introduced them. "This is my brother, Gula Fass and his wife, Malka," and turning back to Mr. and Mrs. Fass, "and these are our friends, Ruth *Kastner* and Calman Mencher."

"Cal," Calman interjected.

"Cal and Ruth are going to be getting married soon." Fass shook hands with Calman and gave a slight bow to Ruth. "In Hungary," he said, my name was Gula Vasserman, but here in Canada everybody shortens their name."

"Yes! So it seems," Calman responded, "but how did you come to the name Fass? I believe that Vasserman means 'a man of the water'. That could mean a sailor, or a fisherman, or simply one who lives near the water. Did you ever attempt to trace the origin of your name?"

"No. We had already changed our name to Vass in Hungary. But when the immigration officer asked me our name He typed in Fass, and I was too tired from all the travelling and running to correct him. Everybody here seems to have a short name, like Smith or Jones."

"Yes, they are common names. Smith means craft. So there used to be a blacksmith, a locksmith, and so on. As for Jones I don't know its derivation. But I would suppose it comes from Johnson, meaning son of John. It is interesting to speculate on name origins."

"And your name is Calman?"

"Yes, but my family and friends call me Cal."

Smiling at Ruth, Emerich said, "I guess we don't have to guess the origin of Ruth's name.

Malka came forward and shook hands with Ruth. "Did you know that Emeric is my brother, but also, that Gula is Helena's brother?"

Ruth chimed in, "So a brother married a sister, and a sister married a brother?"

"Exactly!" said Gula.

Helen, meanwhile, had set the little girl down and busied herself in the kitchen, and Malka followed her. Emeric invited everyone to be seated, and lit up a cigarette. "Calman," he said, "Gula is going into business, manufacturing syrups and raspberry juices, and he will also be importing food products from Hungary and Austria, such as sardines, caviar and dried fruits. If it goes well, he'll expand into other food products, such as salamis, bologna, and wieners."

Gula interrupted, "And I would like to ask you if you would be my accountant."

Calman looked at Stern, "Thank you Mr. Stern for the recommendation," and then turning back to Fass, he said, "It will be a pleasure to set up your financial records and maintain them for you. If you need any advice on banking or other financial matters I'll be available, and, of course, I'll prepare your income tax returns."

Fass asked him, "Do I need to prepare anything for you."

"No," he replied, I'll get you the ledgers and journals, and take care of the rest. After a pause, "When do you expect to commence?"

Fass told him, "I have already leased premises, a warehouse, on Spadina Avenue, near Dundas Street. Do you know where that is?"

"Oh, yes," Calman said, "I'm quite familiar with that district." After another brief lull Calman asked, "Have you decided on a name for your business?"

"We were thinking of Fass Food Products."

"Sounds like a good name," Calman said. "'However, it could be mistaken for Fast Foods."

"So you don't think it's a good idea?" "Well, I think that a name such as 'European Food Imports' might be very appealing both to old-time Canadians as well as new Canadians. What do you think?"

The women were returning pushing a cart containing a variety of pastries and coffee, and they caught Calman's remarks. "Ooh! Yes! I like that name. It's perfect," said Malka, excited at the prospect.

"Yes," said Fass, "that's our new business name, European Food Imports."

"Okay. We'll get the name registered tomorrow," said Calman, "and I'll call on you next Monday morning. Is that all right Mr. Fass?"

"Yes, very good, and please call me Gula, or better still, Julius or Jules," he replied. They exchanged cards and turned their attention to the ladies.

Calman whispered to Ruth: "I see that Mrs. Stern has made strudel. You have never tasted anything quite like it. It's Manna from Heaven."

Helen overheard him and said, "Cal, I've made a little extra strudel for you and packed it in a box. Don't forget to take it with you." Stern brought out a bottle of wine, and started to fill some goblets.

"This," he said, "is special Hungarian wine." Looking at Ruth, he said with a laugh: "You've heard of wine from the Rhine Valley and from the Rhone? This is from the Danube." He handed the adults a glass, and raising his, toasted the young couple: "To our new Canadian friends, Cal and Ruth, on the occasion of their betrothal. May their marriage last long and be filled with many happy events." The oblique glance he made towards Helen did not escape Calman, nor did her sad smile back to him.

"To Cal and Ruth," the others chimed in and clinked glasses.

The little boy had fallen asleep on the rug under a table, and his sister was becoming fidgety and was pulling at her mother's skirt. It was time for the Fass family to leave. They gathered up the children, said their goodbyes and departed. Calman looked at his watch and indicated to Ruth that it was time that they too left. Ruth got up and said to Helen, "Let me help you with the dishes."

"It's really no trouble at all," Helen answered. But Ruth had already loaded a tray and was on her way to the kitchen.

"You know," she told Helen, "I've had lots of experience waitressing. That's how I put myself through university."

Finally, the younger pair started moving towards the door, when Helen called to Ruth. "Just a moment dear, I have a little gift for you," and she brought out a little cloth bag from which she extracted a ruby brooch, which she proceeded to pin on Ruth's blouse.

Ruth gasped, "Oh, Mrs. Stern…Helen…you shouldn't…you…I don't know what to say." Emeric came over, took Ruth's hand, and bent over it brushing it with his lips.

"Cal is a very fortunate man," he said. As they were descending the elevator Ruth said, "They're such lovely people. Would it be all right if we invited them to the wedding?"

Calman smiled: "It would be very all right."

CHAPTER V

Hungary is a land of about thirty-six thousand square miles, located in southeast Europe. It is almost equal in size to Austria which borders it on the west and Czechoslovakia on its northern border and it is more than one-third the size of each of Rumania and Yugoslavia which lie respectively to its east and south. Germany is located at the northern boundary of Austria. The great Danube River, which ranks second only to the Volga among European rivers, divides the land. It runs along the border between Czechoslovakia and Hungary from Bratislava to Esztergom, where it takes a sharp turn south and flows through the great Hungarian plain past Budapest.

The Magyars, a name long associated with the people of Hungary, was a nomadic nation who migrated from the Urals to the Northern Caucasian region in c.460. During the next four hundred years they lived peacefully in an agrarian society. However, late in the ninth century, the Petchenegs, a semi nomadic Turkic people of the Central Asian steppes, forced their way northward into Hungary, compelling the Magyars to become militarized, and they soon became transformed into ferocious warriors mounted on swift horses. Early in the eleventh century the first king of Hungary, St. Stephen, completed the Christianization of the Magyars, and the crown remained the national symbol of Hungarian existence, supported by the Roman Catholic Church for nearly one thousand years thereafter. Francis

Joseph was crowned king of Hungary in 1867, and from that time until the outbreak of World War I, Hungary was one of the most aristocratic and reactionary countries in Europe, controlled by feudal landowners.

There had been a Jewish presence in Hungary dating back to the Roman Empire. However, the status of Jews throughout the centuries was always precarious, and, as in other parts of Europe they were looked down upon with contempt, an object of scorn. Their living conditions were nevertheless bittersweet The persecutions they suffered up to the advent of Nazism in the 1930s were not as severe as in other countries, and despite the restrictions that were imposed on them by the Christian clergy, Hungary was a haven for the Jews. At the end of the eleventh century, although taxed excessively, they were offered protection from the Crusaders by King Koloman.

In the thirteenth century King Bela IV extended them legal rights. And by the fifteenth century large numbers of Jews began settling in Hungary to escape the inquisition, although by the end of the centennial a blood libel broke out resulting in an auto-da-fe against a number of Jews. Then, during the Ottoman regime there was a turn-around again for the Jews. They were allowed to practice their religion freely. But in the following century when the Hapsburgs took control of Hungary the Jewish population was once again oppressed.

In the mid-eighteenth century, during the reign of Maria Theresa, things deteriorated further as Jews were compelled to pay toleration taxes. Thus the history of the Jews in Hungary was one of unpredictable fluctuations, of ups and downs, of twos and fours. Then, once more, in the nineteenth century, the Jewish plight was alleviated, as things took a turn for the better. They were now allowed to settle anywhere in Hungary and they began to play a vital role in commerce, banking and the arts. A number of Jews, especially the successful ones, became aristocrats, if not in title, then in bearing and attitude. They sent their children into the gymnasium instead of the yeshivas, and here in these institutions of learning they were acculturated into the country's elitist values.

They became proud and confident, correct in their business dealings, and authoritarian in the raising of their children. Yet, in the background of their psyche there remained always the fear of another reversal of their collective fortunes. This was the condition of the Hungarian Jews in the year 1897 that saw the birth of Emerich Shternberg and Helena Vasserman.

CHAPTER VI

Rodolfe Shternfeld was born in September, 1875 in the city of Debrecen, located about one hundred miles east of the twin city of Budapest. Pavel Vasserman made his debut onto the planet two months later, in November of that year. It was only two years since the two great cities of Buda and Pest had united, to remain forever seamed by the Danube River. The parents of the two boys shared only a nodding acquaintance and had very little in common. The elder Shternfelds had been born and raised in Hungary, and regarded themselves as Jewish aristocrats.

The Vassermans had emigrated from Poland and were looked upon as outsiders and lower on the social scale of the Jewish community. But fate found the two families living on the same street in the Jewish quarter of Debrecen. In fact they were neighbors, their houses being separated only by a large wooden fence eight feet in height.

Shortly after the Vassermans moved into their new home with their three children, the father called aside his middle child, his only son, eight year old Pavel, and warned him: "Do you see that fence?

"Yes! What's on the other side, Papa?"

"Never mind! You are never to climb it. Do you understand?"

"Yes, Papa. But why?"

"Never mind! I expect you to obey me. If I find you have climbed it you will be punished."

Naturally this admonition only fired the young boy's imagination, and no sooner had his father left the house to attend to his business affairs, than young Pavel commenced his ascent up the fence. As he climbed he felt a rip and looked to find a tear in his trousers which had been caught on a nail, but the damage was done and he was going to be punished anyway, and he only needed two more heaves, and he would be at the top. He continued the climb and reaching the top he straddled the fence. There, on the other side, was a little boy, about Pavel's age, standing feet apart and hands on hips, looking up very cocky at Pavel.

"I've been waiting for you," he challenged. "Come on down on this side, I dare you, and I'll knock you down." Pavel needed no further goading. He jumped and landed on all fours. Immediately the other boy was at him, arms flailing, fists flying. Pavel put out his hands to protect himself, and the other boy ran into his clenched fist. Blood spurted from his nose.

The two boys stopped in astonishment and sized each other up. Then, in a moment, they were at it again, swinging, tripping, and rolling on the ground.

Pavel heard a little girl say, "Rudy, I'm going to tell Mama you're fighting." Within a few moments a heavy-set woman, wearing an apron, came running out, followed by the little girl. The woman pulled the boys apart.

"Rudy," she said, "Papa will hear about this. And who is this little boy?"

"My name is Pavel Vasserman, and I didn't start the fight."

"So! Are you the new neighbors next door?" Pavel nodded. Still holding onto both boys she asked Pavel: "Do you like chocolate cake?" He nodded shyly. "Well then, come on," and she led the way to their house. "This is Rodolfe Shternfeld," and, indicating the girl, "this is his little sister, Bena. Now boys, let me see you shake hands."

The two boys became inseparable companions. They went to the same schools, did their homework together, competed in sports together, and spent much of their time playing together. When both boys were ten an uncle of Pavel came over from England, uncle Mordecai, to visit his relatives in Hungary. He brought with him a gift for his nephew, a large book with a glossy red cover called *Chum*. It contained stories of "The Arabian Nights," "The Arthurian Adventures," and "Robin Hood," together with a number of colored figurations, which spurred the fancy of the young boy. Pavel shared the book with his best friend, and one day proposed: "Let's play Robin Hood."

"All right," said Rodolfe, "but I want to be Robin."

"No, that's not fair," Pavel complained, "The book belongs to me. So, I should be Robin. You can be Little John."

Rodolfe thought about his friend's suggestion and then replied, "No, I won't be that jolly fat man. But I'll tell you what. I'll be King Richard, and you will have to follow my commands and bow down to me."

The elder Shternfeld, Rodolfe's father, had had the good fortune to be apprenticed to a jeweler as a boy, and when he married he opened up a small store with the help of his family, and he and his wife occupied living quarters in the rear. It was here that Rodolfe was born, and that his sister, Bena, was also born and raised until she was six years old, at which time the family moved into a larger house in the Jewish quarter.

The elder Vasserman was raised in a *shtetel* in Poland, and was apprenticed there to a tailor. When Pavel was eight the family emigrated from Poland to Debrecen. The elder Mrs. Vasserman had the reputation of being a superb cook, but she was especially noted for her cherry brandy, which she fermented from the cherries that the family picked off the bushes each summer. As she did not know many people in this new land and found it difficult to cultivate friends, she spent more time in cooking and in brewing vishnik, as the cherry brandy was called. Someone had suggested that she bottle it, and soon her vishnik became a popular aperitif in the community.

The elder Vasserman eventually gave up his tailoring, as he devoted more and more time to his wife's business, which expanded into syrups and other products. When the family felt secure enough they moved into a better section of the city, next to the Shternfelds, who were in the jewelry business.

When Rodolfe was twelve years old his parents decided to leave Debrecen and move to the city of Budapest. For several years the jewelry business had been stagnant, and the elder Shternfeld believed that he had to make the move to the larger city in order for his business to grow. Budapest at that time was the political, cultural, and commercial center of Hungary, and all of his domestic suppliers were located there. Soon after the move Rodolfe was enrolled in a private boarding school, where he received instruction, not only in the academic subjects, but also in the social graces. In short, he was being groomed to become a young gentleman.

Just before his sixteenth birthday Rodolfe was sent off to the gymnasium, which was located some distance away from home, and so he returned home only on holiday seasons. He had grown a little beard and mustache, and had developed an aristocratic demeanor, and had acquired an ebony cane, which he carried with aplomb.

The Vassermans also made the move to Budapest just after Rodolfe had left for the gymnasium, and so the friends were not yet to be reunited. Although Pavel had continued his schooling in Debrecen it did not have the prestige of his friend's private school. After reaching the age of sixteen he came to work in his parents' factory, which now carried a variety of products. Within a short time Pavel had become somewhat of a dandy with the girls, a beau monde, and he had also acquired a cane, which he swung with a carefree gait.

Rodolfe completed his studies at the gymnasium, and returned to Budapest to live in his parents' house. His father sat him down for a man-to-man talk. "Rudy," he commenced, addressing his son by the rarely used nickname, "you have now finished your education. Your older brother, Avrum, as you know, has decided to go into the rabbinate, and I have given him my blessing. You are my only other son, and it is now up to you to carry on the tradition of our business. I want you to come into the jewelry business with me, and on the day you marry I will make you an equal partner."

"Papa, I am very pleased that you have such confidence in me, and it would be an honor to be your partner."

The elder Shternfeld called out to his wife: "Hanna, bring in a bottle of the Vasserman vishnik and two brandy glasses." They sipped the brandy, father and son, and the old man, full of smiles, and gleaming in satisfaction, asked: "So, partner, tell me about this girl, Sarah, whom, I understand, you have been visiting? Is it true that you are courting her?"

The two young men remained friends, but were not as intimate as they had once been. Their personalities had crystallized differently. Pavel was outgoing, extroverted, and ever the romantic. He loved a good tale. Rodolfe was introverted, a rationalist and formal. Although they lived in close proximity to one another, they saw little of each other. In a twist of irony it was their wives who kept up the friendship, and kept the families together.

CHAPTER VII

The summer solstice in the year 1904 was a warm and balmy day, and the Shternberg family and the Vasserman family set out together on a picnic in the country. The Vasserman family was a nuclear unit of four persons – Pavel Vasserman and his wife Greta, and their two Children, Helena who was six and their two-year-old son, Gula. Rodolf Shternberg and his wife Sarah were blessed with three children, seven-year-old Emerich, two-year-old Malka, and an infant barely six months of age, Joseph.

The older children ran on ahead, hand-in-hand, and started down an embankment, towards the Danube. The mothers were behind them. Mrs. Shternberg was pushing the pram containing the sleeping Joseph. "Don't go near the river," called Mrs. Vasserman.

Helena turned to face her, obediently. "Yes, Mama," she called back dutifully. Malka and Gula remained close to their mothers.

The gentlemen strolled a few yards behind. Though it was a sweltering summer day each wore a shirt with tie and elegant pin, a knee-length silk black coat and a fedora. They each also carried a cane. The cane had once served as a weapon, sometimes containing a sword concealed in the shaft. Later as dueling became outlawed it served as a symbol of power and strength. Now it was a token of authority and prestige, and no self-respecting member of the gentry would be seen promenading without his walking stick.

Pavel Vasserman was tall and sinewy, and he was easy-going, always ready to share a joke. His cane had a long shaft and was topped with a dog's head, like a boxer's, made of bone. Rodolfe Shternfeld was a man of smaller stature, and his cane bore an ebonized shaft, with an ivory handle in the form of a hand clenched over a heart. His cane was tipped with a bone ferrule. He wore pince-nez glasses, which pinched the upper part of his nose, and his demeanor was formal, commanding obedience from his underlings and respect from his peers.

Budapest was more than just the capital of Hungary to the two gentlemen. It had become one of the world's great intellectual Jewish centers. Theodor Herzl, the founder of Zionism, was born in Budapest in 1860, and lived in Hungary during his youth. It was during this period that a religious division began to occur in the Jewish community of Hungary, according to two denominations – the Orthodox, the religion as practiced by their forefathers, and the Reform, the new doctrine, which was much more liberal. The Shternfelds and the Vassermans had been raised in the orthodox tradition, but now inclined towards the Reform, even though they retained some of the more conservative practices from the past. "What did you think of the raspberry syrup I sent you last week?" Pavel Vasserman asked his friend Rodolfe Shternfeld as they promenaded along the boardwalk beside the Danube, with their families, on that day of the Summer Solstice.

"You do want my honest opinion, Vasserman, do you not?" Shternfeld asked. He did not mince words. Rodolfe, although reformed in his religion, was conservative in his relationships, and always insisted on decorum. He was formal in dress, in speech and everything else. He always addressed his friend by his surname, and he expected Pavel to address him likewise.

"Yes, Shternfeld…yes, indeed. Tell me the truth."

"Well then, I found it tart."

"Tart?"

"Yes, slightly sharp."

"Aha! You must have tasted it directly from the jar. You are supposed to spread it on a cracker or a slice of bread or a cheese blintz," Vasserman rejoined without a trace of anger.

"All right," Shternfeld remarked, "I will try it with a cracker. But my opinion remains. It is tart…sourish."

"You will love it. Try it on a cracker with some cheese." Shternfeld gave him a look of scorn, and changed the subject.

"What is this I hear that you are expanding your plant? Is it true? Is business that good?"

"Would you believe it, Shternfeld, I cannot keep up with the demand. It is not so long ago that my parents started to produce vishnik. Then we expanded into syrups of all kinds—raspberry, strawberry and so forth. Now I'm looking at selling salamis, knockers and a whole assortment of meat products. We are also going to start producing puddings. There's a big demand for pudding. But this is not all. We are going to start exporting. I am making arrangements with several agents in different countries. The possibilities are enormous."

"Congratulations! I must say that I am surprised at the rate and the scale of your success, and as you know, I wish you all the success.

"Thank you!"

"Tell me, what countries do you have in mind for your products?"

"First, Austria and Germany, and if I do well there I'll spread out to other parts of Europe".

"Do you mind if I give you some advice?"

"I would welcome it."

"Don't expand too quickly, and always make sure that you have capable people representing you, and that you have the financial resources to support the expansion."

They walked hands on in silence for a few minutes. "You know that I have had a lot of business experience, not to belittle your own ability. As I'm sure you also agree, two heads are better than one. So, if you like, I would be glad to go over your plans with you to make sure there are no serious flaws."

"That is very kind of you," Vasserman replied, but he said nothing further for the present. They walked on in silence for a short distance, each immersed in his own thoughts, and then Vasserman asked: "And you, Shternfeld, how is the jewelry business?"

"I don't want to give a *nehora*, but it is going well. My business is also growing, thanks God. Do you remember when I started out the only business I could get came from the Jewish community? Eventually, however, some goyim started to come in. But yesterday I really broke the barrier. A baroness came to the shop in her carriage and ordered a gold watch and chain for the baron."

"A baroness!" Vasserman exclaimed. "That is not only a good omen for your business, but for the whole Jewish community. Are you thinking of branching out like me?"

"No! I may enlarge my store, but I won't open up branches. At least, not in the near future! I'm not as venturesome as you."

"Then how do you expect to grow?"

"My growth comes, not from handling more gold or diamonds, but from changing of styles and settings."

"Well, remember, I'm also available to advise you on your business at any time." Then, as the children ahead caught his eye Vasserman abruptly changed the subject:

"Look over there. My Helena and your Emerich! How pleasing to see them holding hands, like sweethearts. You know, my friend, if you were so inclined I would be amenable now to contracting my daughter in marriage to your son when they become of age. What say you to that, Shternfeld?"

Shternfeld demurred: "I say it is a little early, but I like your proposition. We'll talk about it again soon."

CHAPTER VIII

The year was 1914! Unrest was everywhere. Europe was torn by imperialistic, territorial and economic rivalries. Since the beginning of the twentieth century, hostilities had been intensifying, especially between Great Britain and France against Germany, and between Russia and Austria-Hungary. Then the fireworks were ignited by the assassination of the Archduke Francis Ferdinand of Austria-Hungary at Sarajevo, precipitating the largest conflict in history.

Emeric Shtern…the family name had been shortened for business reasons… was happy. He was seventeen, and a young man in love. He had known Helena since childhood, and years before had been betrothed to her by family arrangement, and they would be married in three years, when both would have reached the age of twenty. He was in attendance at the gymnasium, a classical school preparatory for university, where he would be studying engineering science. This was the very school his father, Rodolfe, had attended twenty years earlier. Emerich was a good student and excelled in Latin, history and mathematics, but his standing was secured when he became the school's chess champion. For three years now he remained undefeated, and was preparing to represent the school in the national competitions. He held the respect, not only of his peers but also of the schoolmasters. The family thought it best if he lived in residence at the gymnasium which was located about twenty miles north of

Budapest. They looked forward to every other weekend, when he would return home to his family and sweetheart.

Helena was also an exceptionally good student and was attending an academy where her concentration was art and design. Now that Helena was affianced to Emerich she customarily joined the Shtern family for the traditional Friday evening dinner when Emerich would return home for his bimonthly visit. One evening she arrived at the Shtern home as usual, and Sabbath greetings were exchanged. The officious Mr. Rodolfe Shtern shook her hand, and Mrs. Shtern, his affectionate wife and the most demonstrative member of the household, clasped her and kissed her on the cheek. Helena breathed in the aroma of cooking and baking, and felt comfortable and at ease with the family.

"Has Emerich arrived home yet?" Helena asked.

"No, he is usually home by this time," Mrs. Shtern commented, "but tonight he seems to be running a little late."

Malka came over to Helena and took her hand, "Let's wait in my room. I would like you to see my latest drawings." Up they flew, two steps at a time.

"How is Gula?" she asked Helena.

"Oh, he's fine. He has exams coming up. So he's studying hard. He's anxious to do well."

"Well, you can give him my regards, and after he has completed his exams bring him with you on one of your visits to our home."

"Malka, he'll be pleased that you were asking about him, and I know that he'll be looking forward to joining your family on a Sabbath evening. Now let me see your drawings."

Half an hour had elapsed, and Mrs. Shtern approached her husband: "Rudy, it's getting dark out. He's never been this late before. What do you think could have happened?"

"Now, now, nothing has happened Sarah," he tried to assure her. "The train must have just been delayed. He'll be home any minute," but the quiver in his voice betrayed his own anxiety.

Joseph, who was now a young man of nearly twelve, said, "I'm getting hungry. Why can't we start eating?" But the conversation slowed down and gave way to a tense silence. The girls came out of Malka's room and descended the stairs slowly.

Helena went up to Mrs. Shtern and touched her arm. "What do you think might have happened? Could he have forgotten that this was the weekend he was due home?"

Mrs. Shtern reached out to her comfortingly, and assured her: "No, no, Helena dear, we think that the train was delayed. I'm sure he'll be here soon."

Shtern pulled out his pocket watch and saw that the hour had passed. He put on his hat and took up his walking stick. "I'm going out to look for him."

"No!" his wife entreated him, grasping his arm, "Where will you go in this black night? Emerich will be here soon. You said so yourself."

"All right!" reason prevailed. "We will give him fifteen minutes more and then we will proceed with the Shabbas dinner."

At the end of fifteen minutes precisely the punctilious Mr. Rodolfe Shtern peremptorily announced, "It is now Shabbas. Light the candles." Mrs. Shtern and the two girls placed a white brocaded silk kerchief over each of their heads, and standing before the lighted candelabra, one girl on each side of her, she extended her arms and recited the traditional blessing:

"Baruch ato adoinoi… lehadlik ner shell Shabbas."

The dinner was eaten in silence, and the evening passed without a word from Emerich. When dinner had ended, Shtern escorted Helena the two blocks to her door. No word was exchanged during the walk, but when they arrived at the house, Shtern bid her goodnight and said to her, "Please convey my regards to your parents, and wish them for me a Good Sabbath."

"Won't you come in?" she offered, "I think that Papa would want to talk to you."

"Not tonight," he said crisply and was gone. Helena rushed up the few stairs, and when her mother opened the door for her she fell into her arms sobbing.

"Open up!" there was a pounding at the door!"

"Just a moment," called Sarah Shtern as she rushed to open the door. It was Pavel Vasserman.

"What has happened to Emerich?" Vasserman demanded, as if there was a conspiracy against him. An ashen Shtern came forward and stood beside his wife.

"Come in, Pavel." He hadn't called him by his given name since their childhood days. "Emeric did not come home from the gymnasium. We have no idea what could have happened."

"This is very serious. Come, I will go with you to the police station." The two friends walked over to the depot and spoke to the officer in charge.

"This is a very common occurrence," he explained. "It happens all the time."

"Is their nothing you can do," Shtern cried.

"No," said the officer, "In the first place we do not know if your son is in fact missing. So you cannot file a missing person's complaint. You must wait a few days, and in the second place it did not occur in this jurisdiction."

"Then there is nothing you can do."

"I advise you to go home and get a good night's sleep. By morning everything will be resolved. It usually is." The two friends returned to their homes.

Shtern did not go to sleep that night. All night long he sat in his rocker and rocked. Wearing his black silk coat, his pince-nez pinching his nose, he rocked to and fro. His wife brought him a blanket and a cup of tea. He drank the tea wordlessly, and he rocked. He waited and he rocked. At daybreak he rose, put on a gray tweed jacket, donned his gray felt hat with the curled brim, lifted his ebony cane from its stand and departed from the house.

Shtern walked doggedly across the city, arriving finally at the railroad station. He sat down on a hard wooden bench, and remained there for some time as though in a trance. Finally he got up and went to the wicket. "What time does the train leave for Szomsathely?" he enquired.

"Half an hour," the clerk replied tersely.

"Give me a return ticket." He had decided to seek advice from his older brother, Avrom Shtern, the rabbi of Szomsathely, a town about one hundred miles from Budapest.

The brothers sat together in the rabbi's study and sipped the tea the rabbi's wife had brought them. "Start from the beginning," The older man said. "Tell me exactly what happened."

"There is nothing to tell. Emerich was supposed to come home last night to join us in a Sabbath meal and to return to the gymnasium on Sunday, but he did not appear. He has never been late before. We are all very worried that something evil has befallen him."

"All right now! We have to keep our heads. The rabbi stroked his beard in thought. "The first thing you must do," he said, "is go to the gymnasium and see if Emerich is still there."

"What would he be doing there?"

"Who knows? Perhaps he made a mistake about the weekend he was to come home."

Shtern interrupted: "Emerich never makes such mistakes."

45

The brother retorted: "There could be many reasons. Perhaps he had to study for an exam and could not reach you."

In the silence that followed the rabbi felt embarrassed by his own insipid explanations. Then, in a conciliatory tone: "Perhaps he is ill." There was another long silence. "Yes," said the rabbi decisively, "he could be ill or have had an accident, and they have no means of reaching you. You must leave immediately for the school. If he is not there, speak to the principal and his teachers, speak to his friends." Shtern got up to leave.

"Wait! I'm coming with you."

Shtern looked at his brother quizzically, "Will you drive with me on the Sabbath?"

"God always allows for special dispensations in emergencies." As they left the house, the rabbi gave instructions to his wife: "Take Herzl with you and go to my brother's home. Stay with Sarah and comfort her until you hear from us."

CHAPTER IX

When the brothers arrived at the school it was already sundown. They entered the main building and immediately noticed two young men strolling in the corridor. They approached the boys who regarded them with surprise.

The younger brother spoke:

"Good evening young gentlemen. Would you happen to be acquainted with a student by the name of Emerich Shtern?"

The bolder of the two boys replied. "I don't know him personally, but I know who he is. He's the school chess champion."

A momentary look of pride lighted up Rodolfe Shtern's countenance. "Could you tell us where we could find him?"

"No! But we could show you to the dormitory where he shares a room." The boys lighted up their lanterns and guided the two men to the dorm where they quickly found Emerich's quarters. They opened the door abruptly and interrupted a young man reading. The lad jumped up taken by surprise.

"We're sorry to disturb you in your studies, but we are looking for your room-mate."

"You mean Emerich Shtern?

"Yes! Have you seen him?"

"He went home for the weekend, and is not expected back until tomorrow. Is something wrong?"

"I am Mr. Shtern, Emerich's father. Emerich did not arrive home last night. I have come here to find out what has happened. Are you certain he left for home?"

"Well, he packed a satchel, same always and took two books. He waved to me from the door, and said he would be back by late afternoon tomorrow."

"Can you tell us where the principal lives?"

"I don't know, Sir."

The men withdrew to the hallway to consult. The boy followed. "Do you think something has happened?" the boy asked, visibly shaken.

"We don't know. That is what we are trying to find out." After a few solemn moments of hesitation the men started towards the door.

"Oh, Sir!" the young man called after them, "Perhaps you would like to see the headmaster. His rooms are in this building."

The headmaster was apologetic as he served them with scones and tea. "I'm afraid this is all I can offer you at this late hour."

They thanked him: "You are most generous."

He had already sent a school monitor to the principal's home to notify him of the emergency. The young man who shared the room with Emerich remained in the headmaster's quarters, and the headmaster now began to question him.

"Stephen, how well do you know Emerich?"

"We share the same room. His bed is the one next to the window; mine is on the other side by the wall. His desk is always neat. In fact he is always neat and well groomed. He's a very good student and sometimes he helps me with my homework. But we don't have our meals together. I have my own group of friends."

"And can you tell us anything about his habits? Who are his friends? Does he ever go into town?"

"Well," the boy drawled, "He's very quiet and he reads a lot. I don't know if he has many friends, except maybe from the chess club."

"You know that he goes home on every second weekend though?"

"Yes, Sir!"

"Does he ever travel home with other boys from the school?"

"I don't know. Sometimes he shares a hansom to the train station."

"Do you know with whom?"

"Well, there's Wilhelm." "There are several Wilhelms. Which one would that be?

"I don't know, Sir."

The headmaster dismissed the boy, "Thank you, Stephen; you have been most helpful. You may return to your quarters for the present."

As the boy was leaving, an agitated principal rushed into the room, accompanied by a police inspector. He turned to Shtern: "Are you Emerich's father?" "I am his father and this is his uncle." There was a perfunctory handshake. "This is most distressing. From the very inception of this institution we have never lost a student under such circumstances. Now two students have disappeared." "Who is the other student?" asked the headmaster? "His name is Wilhelm Kurtiss." The inspector stepped in:

"We have learned that the two boys rented a hansom, and that they travelled together to the railway station. We also know that they arrived at the station, paid the hansom driver, and got out of the cab together.

The principal interrupted: "We found the hansom driver and interrogated him. We obtained this information from him."

The inspector continued: "We have also learned that neither boy pur-
chased a railway ticket. From this information we can infer two things:
firstly, that they are together; and, second, that they are within the vicinity.
We can make a third inference: Because of the family backgrounds of
both boys and their school records, it is unlikely that they would run off.
Therefore, we conclude that they must have met with foul play. However,
because there are two of them they may have been able to ward off their
attackers. They may be injured, or they may be in hiding, or both. We shall
scour the countryside until we find them and return them safely home.

The elder Shtern asked: "What can we do in the meantime? We are
very worried."

"We have told Wilhelm's family the same. There is nothing you can do.
We have an excellent constabulary, and they are combing every inch of
ground around the station as well as the wider vicinity. You will be notified
as soon as they are found."

CHAPTER X

Joseph was standing at the casement looking out the window. "Look, Mama! Look at the snow."

Mrs. Shtern came to the window. "Goodness me! It's very early for snow. It usually does not start snowing until the middle of December. And Malka is outside without her snowshoes." They watched the snow cascading down, fascinated by the rhythm.

"Joseph," she said to her youngest son, "I want you to dress warmly, take your sister's winter coat and galoshes, and go out and find her. Tell her that she must return home with you immediately."

He left on his errand, but did not return for hours. When he returned home finally, he was admonished: "And where have you been you truant?"

"Oh! Gee! We were having a snowball fight. It was so much fun, Mama."

"And what happened to your sister? Did you forget about her?"

"Oh! I forgot. I'm sorry. I'll go get her right away."

"Never you mind! She's been home for hours."

"And do you remember where you left her coat and overshoes?"

"I guess I put them down somewhere. But I know where I left them. I'll get them right away."

"You're very lucky. Your friend Marcus, who is more responsible than you are, brought them home. Now go to your room, and get out of those wet clothes."

"Could I have a cookie?"

"No! Your father is going to hear about this."

That winter the snow rose to unprecedented heights, and the children screamed with glee as they jumped from roof tops into the snow piles below.

The cruel spring came with a torrent of melting snow and flooded the countryside. The water levels rose and the rivers overflowed their banks, and the Danube disgorged the body of Wilhelm Kurtiss. Immediately a search was launched for the body of Emerich Shtern along the banks of the Danube, but the river would not yield up any more prizes. The Shtern family, friends and neighbors teamed up and searched along the shores and the environs. Nothing! Not a clue! Gradually they all drifted back to their normal lives, all but Rodolfe Shtern. He alone continued, day after day, to explore meticulously every furrow, every cranny along the banks, and he kept returning to the same spots he had already surveyed only to recommence his search again and again, a veritable Sisyphus, attempting vainly to climb out of his mental morass. He carried with him a talisman, the white king of his son's chess set, as a good luck token, hoping desperately to discover some small sign of his son. He returned to the police inspector, who was very patient with him:

"Will you comb the river again, just one more time please?"

"Now, see here, Mr. Shtern, we have done all we can. Yours is not the only case, and we have others to solve. If we learn anything we will notify you at once." As if to emphasize that the case was closed, as far as the police were concerned the inspector shut the file that lay open on his desktop and consigned it to a drawer.

Finally, the once proud and immaculate gentleman, reduced now to an exhausted and disheveled relic, was brought home by the police. Mrs. Shtern was warned, "He has become a nuisance and is interfering with our own investigation. If we find him wandering around the banks again he will be arrested."

"Yes! Yes! Officers, I assure you it won't happen again," and she led her husband upstairs to their bedroom. He lay down on the bed, and she untied his shoelaces, took off his shoes, and covered him with a warm blanket. She quietly closed the door and went downstairs to brew some tea for him.

A few days passed. Shtern was not attending to business. His clothes hung loosely on him, and he had not trimmed his beard. He left the house and disappeared for the entire day.

"Did you see Papa leave the house?" Sarah asked the children. "Did you hear him say where he was going?" They hadn't. She placed a shawl on her shoulders and walked hurriedly over to the Vassermans, accompanied by her younger son, Joseph.

"Greta," she said to Pavel's wife, "Rodolfe has disappeared. He left the house hours ago in a confused state." She daren't say the word 'mad'. If the police find him wandering around the riverbank they will arrest him. I am distraught with worry."

Gula, who was standing by and heard the conversation, said: "I'll go look for him."

"No, you won't," said his mother. "Go to the plant, and fetch your father. Run!" Pavel came running to the house breathless, followed by his son.

"What happened?" Sarah recounted to him the events of the last few days.

"Emerich was his pride and joy," Pavel remarked. Joseph shifted uneasily from one foot to the other. "I think he has gone mad with grief. I'm going out to find him. Joseph, you stay with your mother and look after her. Gula, you come with me."

Rodolfe Shtern left his manorial home, unkempt and distracted, and commenced wandering. He had always prided himself on his neatness, his rationality and his efficiency, habits that he had acquired years ago at the university. But on this day his mind was in disarray. He was mad. His madness was that he was going against his second nature. He was not wandering aimlessly. That would have been a symptom of depression, but not insanity. But he was very clear on his destination. Therefore he was mad. He was heading towards the Roma district of Budapest, where the gypsies dwelt.

Rodolfe arrived eventually at the Roma ghetto, home of the outcasts. His eye took in the squalor of the surroundings, the cramped living conditions, the dwellings on wheels, the vagabondage, the vulnerability of the people. The children wondered: "Who was this stranger in their midst?" A woman wearing a gaudy skirt that flared out and a bandana sat on a crate holding a deck of cards. Rodolfe approached her.

"Are you a diviner?" he asked her in a voice barely louder than a whisper.

"A what?"

"A diviner, you know, a fortune-teller."

"You want your fortune told?"

"Yes."

"Just a minute! Hey! Samru." A portly man stepped out of the caravan and looked quizzically at the woman and her visitor. "This gentleman wants his fortune told."

"Please, come this way." He motioned for Shtern to enter the caravan. They sat down facing each other. "You have to pay me first." Shtern pulled some coins out of his pocket. The man made no offer to pick up the coins.

"Is that not enough?" Shtern pulled out more coins and tossed them on the table.

The man nodded and smiled, and picked up the money. "Put out your hand."

Shtern reached out the left hand. "Are you left-handed?"

"No! I'm right-handed." The man indicated his right hand, and Shtern shifted. The man took hold of Shtern's hand and held it, palm up.

"Hmm!" he studied the palm. "Do you see this line?" he said, tracing it with his finger. "It means you will have a long life. But do you see this shorter line, which comes from your line. This could be a child or someone very close to you. That life will be cut short." Gazing into the grief-stricken face of Shtern, he guessed: "Yes, this person has now passed over to the other side."

Shtern rose, and turned to leave; then stopped and faced the rustic again. "Is there someone here who can read cards?"

"I can!"

"Thank you! But I need someone else."

"Stay here. I will bring you someone." He sat down again, and in a few minutes a woman entered. She had a deck of cards with her. No word passed between them. She mixed the cards then spread them out in a half moon. She motioned to him to take a card. He selected. It was the king of diamonds.

"That must be me," he mused to himself. "I deal in diamonds." She pointed again. He selected again and turned the card over. Jack of spades! He gasped and she stood up. He dropped the remainder of the coins he had on the table, and left hurriedly. Once out of the compound he stopped, and seeing that no one was around, he wept quietly.

Shtern started the trek back, and as he came within a few blocks from his home he ran into Vasserman and his son. Vasserman saw the grief-stricken face of his friend, and threw his arms around him. "My dear friend, Rudy, I grieve for you to see you suffering so much."

"Pavel, my son is dead."

Gula let out a cry. "How do you know this? Has he been found?"

"No! But I know it."

"How? How do you know?" Vasserman repeated.

"From the gypsies!"

Pavel looked at him in astonishment. *My friend has gone mad*, he thought.

A few days later Shtern's brother, Avrum, and his wife, Hanna, came to pay him a visit. "Rodolfe," the rabbi spoke softly but severely, "you must control yourself. Stop these obsessions, first with the river, and now with the gypsies. At this moment we do not know what has befallen Emerich."

"Yes, Avrum," Shtern replied. "Six months have now passed. What should we do? The police already have closed the file, and they presume my Emerich dead." Wringing his hands, he continued, "Do you think we should now go into formal mourning and say our farewells? The waiting is taking a heavy toll off my wife. And I cannot concentrate on my business."

The rabbi replied solemnly: "To a Jew every life is sacred. Whether your son is alive or not his soul is under God's protection."

"But is it not decreed that a family of one deceased must say the Kadish, the prayer for the dead?"

"Yes, but we do not yet know if he is in fact dead."

"Then what if he is never found? Do we never pray for his soul?" And the rabbi replied:

"After four seasons have passed from the day he disappeared, if you have had no sign that he may be alive, then you will wait a further sixty days, and then you will recite the Kadish, but until then you must not abandon hope."

On the train returning to Szombathely the rabbi's wife asked him: "Tell me husband and rabbi, in your heart of hearts do you believe Emerich is alive?"

"My dear wife," he answered her, "my heart believes that the boy lives, but my mind tells me that he sleeps in the river."

Shtern, who had been a Reform Jew most of his life, returned to the Orthodoxy of his father, and joined the Dohany Street Synagogue. He had not worn the phylacteries since his youth, but now he strapped the little black boxes containing strips of parchment, inscribed with verses from the scriptures, to his forehead and his left arm and recited the morning prayers. He prayed to God:

"Spare my son, return him whole, and I will pray to you every day for the remainder of my days. Amen."

Helena, too, acted out the ritual of coming to the Shtern household every alternate Friday evening for the Sabbath dinner. She had recurring dreams that one Friday evening she would arrive at the Shtern home and that she would be greeted by Emerich.

CHAPTER XI

The spring passed, and the summer passed, and autumn was under way, and it was the second day before the Jews of Budapest would celebrate the holiest day of the year, Rosh Hashanah, the Jewish New Year, when the envelope arrived at the Shtern home. Shtern had now recovered his composure and was occupied at his desk, checking accounts, reviewing invoices and attending to other administrative matters concerning the business. The envelope was dirty and creased, and had a rank odor. The address was barely legible, written in a shaky hand. The crinkled envelope rested on the edge of Shtern's otherwise meticulous desk, and he left it until all other matters had been given his attention. Finally he picked it up with his fingertips, and, turning his nose away, quickly slit it open. He withdrew two pages, which had writing on both sides, and examined the scrawl. He noted that the letter was dated as of three months previous. But the scribble was so bad he had great difficulty following it.

He was about to consign it to the wastebasket, when something in the letter caught his attention; perhaps it was the style, the way the letter T was crossed. He started reading the letter again. Suddenly he had the sensation of one drowning in a whirlpool, plunging in and around a sea of foam, and then silence. All was tranquil, and he realized that he lay on the floor in a faint. He tried to call out, but his voice was dead. He pulled himself up and grasping the paper he stumbled into the kitchen, where his wife and Malka were baking, and emitted a hoarse scream, waving the crumpled letter at them. "Where is Joseph?"

But Joseph had already heard the commotion and had come running: "What is it, Papa?"

He could only wave the paper. Then, from the depths of his throat, from the crater of his being, he released a mixture of a howl, a cry and a laugh, and rasped out two indistinct words: "He lives."

Shtern succumbed into his old rocker, and gave way to uncontrolled weeping. Joseph stood behind him and rested a hand on his father's shoulder. He had never before touched his father so intimately, and now, he too began to cry. Mother and daughter in shock, moved forward, and soon all four were entangled in an embrace, weeping and laughing convulsively. When Shtern was finally composed he said to Joseph, "Quickly, run over to the Vasserman family and tell them the good news."

"But," Joseph complained, "Can't I hear what Emerich has written first?"

"Yes, of course. But then you'll go."

My Beloved Family:

I am writing you from a large tent, which is a makeshift hospital. A kindhearted nurse gave me some writing paper and a pen, and promised to send this letter to you. I am in the hospital because I was wounded in battle, but I will recover.

I left the gymnasium last September with a friend to come home for the weekend. We hired a hansom to take us to the railway station. But we no sooner arrived and paid the driver than a gang of thugs dressed in soldiers' uniforms waylaid us. We were badly beaten and tossed into a wagon, which contained four other boys, also severely beaten. We were driven for some time along bumpy roads beside the Danube. When the wagon slowed down my school chum seized the opportunity to jump out, and ran for his life. The soldiers didn't even try to stop him. They aimed their rifles and shot him, and threw his body into the river. They then warned us: "The same will happen to you if you try to escape."

We traveled for several hours, stopping only for short intervals to let the horses rest. Finally, we arrived at a small village where we were ordered into a barn. We were cold, hungry and scared. About a dozen other young men, some of whom were bloodied, occupied the barn; others had their hands tied behind their backs. There was a stove near where I was standing, and it gave off some heat and I managed to edge closer to it unnoticed. In the center of the barn was a table, behind which sat a German army officer. We were all made to stand at attention in front of the officer who addressed us in German, but I could not follow his dialect, and missed most of what he said. At the end of his speech we were made to raise our right hand and swear an oath. Then another officer spoke to us in Hungarian. "Congratulations," he said, "You are now in the German army. If you obey your officers, you may live to return home after we have won the war. But if you disobey orders or try to escape or leave your post without permission you will be hunted down and shot by a firing squad.

The next day we were given uniforms and a rifle, and we were piled into wagons and herded across the border. We were sent to a training camp where we were taught to use a rifle and bayonet. We were forbidden to contact anyone outside the camp. The boys who were in the first wagon with me became my comrades especially since we were in the same platoon. I am not quite sure where we are, except that it is either France or near the French border. We are in the trenches and life here is grueling. Several of the men in our unit have died of typhoid, the food is badly cooked and unappetizing, the chill and dampness penetrates our bones, but we survive through humor, like mimicking our officers, and by singing bawdy songs. When the order comes to charge we fix our bayonets and rush over the parapet to face the enemy, who are just as scared as we. The officers shoot those of us who hesitate. Two of my comrades were killed in the field, I was the third to go down, shot in the leg. One of my comrades carried me out of the line of fire and saved my life. I will be sent back to the front as soon as my wound heals. I look forward to the day when we may all be united again. However, please do not attempt to reach me. It is too dangerous. I will write to you again as soon as possible. However, if you do not hear from me for six months you will know that I am dead. I do not fear death anymore. I am beyond that now. Do not forget me. Pray for me.

One more thing! Please tell my lovely Helena that I release her from her vow. If I should return, she will not recognize the animal I have become.

Your ever-loving son and brother

Emerich

CHAPTER XII

April 1959 was a hectic month for Calman Mencher and Company, Chartered Accountants, as it was for most accounting firms. His practice had grown substantially since the day he started in 1948, and he now employed nine personnel, including two articling students. All income tax returns had to be completed, checked by Calman himself, and filed by the deadline, April 30th. It was now half way through the month and the stragglers kept arriving in a never-ending stream, most of their records in a mess. Calman worked five days a week until 10 p.m. and on Saturdays to 6 p.m. And when he returned home on Saturday evening it was with a packed briefcase. Ruth was critical of him.

"Cal," she complained, "you are working yourself into a state of collapse. You have become irritable and the children don't know you anymore. When is this going to end? And I want to know what you're going to do about it?"

"I know, I know," he said, "but it will all be over in two weeks, and then I promise we'll go away for a few days. What do you say we take a five-day cruise?"

"I'm not worried about myself. I'm concerned about you."

"O.K. Let's take in a movie tonight."

"No! You'll be fidgeting all evening, balancing numbers in your head. Just try to find a way in the future where you can spread out the work over a longer period or pass on some responsibility to your juniors, or perhaps you should begin thinking of taking in a partner." Calman knew that it was futile to argue, so he muttered "hmph!" and let it go at that.

Calman had worked on Sunday until midnight, but the next day he was up, shaved, breakfasted and was on his way to the office by 8:30 A.M. He reflected: *It's a good thing I'm under forty and strong. How does a man of fifty get through this frenetic pace? There must be a better way to process tax returns. What if the deadline for filing tax returns were spread out according to the individual's birthday? Nope! This would not work out.*

He arrived at the office, and nodded to Audrey, the receptionist. She followed him into his office. "I've got some hot coffee brewing. Would like some?"

"Yes, thanks. And ask Shelly to come in when he arrives."

She nodded, "and by the way," she announced, "a Mr. Edward Peterson from the tax department called you."

Calman murmured:

"Who the hell is he, and why does he bother me in April?" The staff had placed several files on his desk for review, and he commenced going through them. Shelly arrived and remained standing. Calman started in without even glancing at Shelly: "Did you prepare these returns for Paul Barton?"

"Yeah!"

"What do you mean 'yeah'? The word is 'yes'. Professional people don't use that kind of slang. Do you understand?"

"Yeah!.....sure." Calman threw him a glance of annoyance.

Shelly interjected: "I mean yes."

Calman shoved the file he had been reviewing to Shelly, and said impatiently: "Luckily for you, this is not an examination room, or you would fail."

"Gee! What did I do wrong?"

Calman said with exasperation: "You know, between your 'yeahs' and your 'gees' it's a good thing you're not an English major. Now, you want to know what you've done wrong? Well, you've only made one mistake as far as I can see. The net income you are reporting is wrong. Do you know why?" Shelly gave him a look of unbelief. "Let me tell you why. The Statement of Income and Expenses does not add up." He gave the young man a withering look. "Take the file back and make the corrections, and then return it to me." As Shelly was leaving the room, Calman called after him, "And I thought I told you to get a haircut." As the articling student exited Calman thought: *He's got to go. I haven't got the time to spoonfeed him. After tax-time I'll hire a graduate.*

The intercom buzzed. "Yes, Audrey?"

"Mr. Peterson is on the line."

"Damn," Calman muttered and picked up the line, "Hello!"

"Hello, Mr. Mencher? This is Edward Peterson, Department of National Revenue." The voice over the phone was young and thin. Immediately and instinctively Calman appraised his character—a neophyte, someone still wet behind the ears, a smart-alec kid looking to make trouble. However, he had learned his lesson well from Vincent Stanton. Never look down on civil servants, especially tax auditors. You never know what grudges lurk in their souls. So, affecting his most courteous tone he remarked:

"Have we met before? Your name has a familiar ring."

"No, I don't think so." The reply was formal and aloof. The man was all business. There would be no small talk with this guy. Besides, Calman noticed the large number of tax files on his desk waiting for his review. He himself did not have the time for pleasantries right now.

So he plunged onward. "Well, now, Mr. Peterson, what is the purpose of your call?"

"I am calling to enquire whether you have a client by the name of Julius Fass."

"Yes, I do." The curt response was as much a question as an answer.

"I would like to examine Mr. Fass's bank passbook."

Calman was incredulous: "Did you say 'his passbook'? I don't believe he has any bank account other than the current account he uses for his business—European Food Imports. All his personal expenses are paid out of that account and, I can assure you, they are charged to his personal drawing account. Is that what you want to see? If so, let me tell you that this man only manages to eke out a living from his business and nothing more. Why would you be investigating him?"

"Sir," Peterson got in, "with great respect, my supervisor has asked me to enquire after his bank passbook. At present I have no interest in his company, European Food Imports, although our present enquiries may lead to an investigation of that company."

The voice was now belligerent and threatening. Calman thought, "This guy's got a chip on his shoulder. I'd better placate the son-of-a-bitch."

"All right," he said, "I'll call him and ask him to make his passbook available for your inspection, but I would be very surprised to learn that such a book exists. Let me have your phone number, and I'll get back to you."

Calman buzzed Audrey. "Yes, Mr. Mencher."

"Ask Shelly to come in, and get me Mr. Fass."

"Shelly's gone for a haircut. I'll get Mr. Fass for you." Click!

"Gone for a haircut," Calman muttered in exasperation, "and on my time. He'll probably give me the excuse that his hair grows on my time." He smiled in amusement at the joke. The line buzzed: "Yes!"

"I've got Mr. Fass for you."

"Thanks." He switched to the other line: "Hello Jules?"

"Hello, Mr. Mencher. Did you want to speak to me?"

"Yes. I've got some good news for you. Your income tax returns are ready, and you have no tax to pay. In fact you get a slight refund."

"Thank you. That's good news."

"Is there any chance, Jules, that you could drop in to sign the returns as we're very close to the deadline and I don't want to take a chance on mailing them, since they may arrive late?"

"Yes, of course. It's no problem. I'll come by on Wednesday."

"Good! By the way, do you happen to have a bank passbook?"

"Yah! I do."

"Do you happen to have it handy there?"

"Yah! Just a minute I think it's in the desk drawer. Yah! I have it here."

"Now would you mind opening it up and telling me what your balance is at present?"

A moment passed, and then: "I have as of two days ago sixteen dollars and eight cents. I've not made any deposits since."

"Very good," Calman said, relieved, "when you come in on Wednesday would you mind bringing the passbook with you?" Calman hung up the phone and was inclined to phone up Peterson and remonstrate with him, but just then Shelly walked in.

On Wednesday morning Calman was seated at his desk immersed in files. He picked up the first file, scanned the top page, and then flipped to the next page. He scanned that page too, and then flipped to the next. He repeated this procedure until he had examined the entire file. And then, pleased, he closed the file, and, using a green led-pencil, placed a check-mark on the folder at the top right-hand corner, and initialled it, making a mental note of the clerk who had prepared the file, so that he could commend him later. He then picked up the second file.

Audrey buzzed Calman: "Mr. Fass is here."

"Good! Show him in."

She led the gentleman into Calman's office and asked him: "Would you care for a cup of coffee Mr. Fass?"

He declined: "Someday, Miss, I will invite you to visit me at my office, and I will prepare a cup of real coffee for you. Then you will understand why we Europeans cannot drink this stuff you call 'coffee'."

Calman smiled and addressed Fass:

"Sit down Jules." He opened a drawer in his desk and withdrew a large manila envelope, from which he extracted Fass's tax return: "Here you are, Jules; just sign where I have marked an x." He handed his pen to Fass who signed the form as directed. "We'll send it out for you," and he handed Fass another envelope. "This is your copy." Fass took the envelope, and Calman asked him casually: "By the way, did you remember to bring the bank passbook?" Fass put his hand into the breast pocket of his jacket and withdrew the little book. Calman accepted the passbook and turned immediately to the last entry in the book and noted that the balance was sixteen dollars and eight cents, exactly as Fass had told him.

But something else caught his attention, and his heart skipped a beat. He then placed a lined sheet of paper on the desk and began writing rapidly, copying entries from the passbook. He prepared four lists of amounts, headed respectively from left to right, 1956, 1957, 1958, and 1959 and then he added each list. "Jules," he said, "I see that in the year 1956 you deposited almost seven million dollars in this account; in 1957 you deposited about eleven million dollars; in 1958 sixteen million, and so far this year six million seven hundred and ninety-two dollars." After a long pause, "What's going on?"

"I don't understand," Fass replied innocently, "What do you mean, 'What's going on'? What should be going on?"

Calman looked him squarely in the eye: "This is a great deal of money. It is important that I know where it came from."

"Tell me," said Fass, "how did you find out about the passbook?"

"I received a call from the income tax department, a fellow by the name of Peterson. He told me about the existence of your savings account and he wanted to examine the passbook. I thought he was mad, but now I see why he was so insistent."

"How did he find out about the account?" Fass wanted to know.

"I have no idea. Probably someone from your bank noticed the large sums being deposited, and notified the department or the R.C.M.P."

"Why is it his business to know where my money comes from? I thought this is a free country."

"If the moneys deposited came from income earned in Canada it should have been reported on your income tax returns, and so it is his business. If it came from some unlawful act, such as drug dealing, the police will be doing the investigating." Fass thought for a while, and then pulled a pack of Luckies from his pocket and extracted a cigarette. He fumbled for a match, and Calman leaned forward with his lighter. Fass took a long puff, and Calman took the opportunity to fill his pipe with an aromatic tobacco, tamp it down, and light up.

"All right," Fass said, "The explanation is very simple. I just don't think it's anybody's business. As you know my wife, Malka is Emerich Shtern's sister, and they come from a wealthy family of retail jewelers. Before Emeric and his wife Helen, who, as you also know, is my sister, immigrated to Canada, they liquidated the business in Hungary, but there was still a lot of inventory on hand. We divided it up, half to them and half to us. When we came to Canada we each brought our jewelry with us, and for the past three years we've been selling it off. That's the whole story."

Calman was skeptical: "And do these deposits which represent the proceeds from the sale of your jewelry include the Stern's share?"

"Yes, absolutely!"

"So tell me, when you entered Canada did you declare your jewelry to customs?" "

Did I declare the jewelry to the customs? At the moment I can't remember. Were we supposed to?"

"I'm sure that Mr. Peterson already knows whether you did or did not." Calman's language now changed from the affable and informal style to the professional and formal. "You understand, sir, that this is not a game. There are serious penalties for lying to the government. Now, you are my client, and I am here to protect you, but I cannot be of any help unless I have all the facts. So here is what I require. First, how much, if any, did you report to customs? If you do not know ask Mr. Stern. He's pretty meticulous about keeping records. Second, I want to see a list showing the names and addresses of all the people to whom you made these sales, and the amounts they paid. And third, I want to know to whom you paid moneys out of your savings account. Do you think you can provide me with this information?"

"Yes, of course Mr. Mencher," a chastised Gula responded.

"All right, when can I have it?"

"Would tomorrow be all right?

The next day Cal was too busy to notice that Fass had not come in with the information, until he received a call from Peterson. He was forced to lie: "I'm sorry, but I've been very busy and have not had an opportunity to see Mr. Fass. You'll have to wait until the end of the month."

"No I don't," Peterson was annoyed.

"Look here," Calman was now allowing his anger to show, "I think that for some reason of your own you're bent on harassing me and my client. You know very well that the filing deadline expires in ten days, and that I cannot give this matter my attention right now."

"All right, I'll go directly to Mr. Fass. I don't have to come to you at all."

"I have a much better idea, Mr. Peterson. Give me the name of your supervisor and his phone number." He had called Peterson's bluff and the man grudgingly agreed to wait until the beginning of May. Calman immediately phoned up Fass. An unfamiliar voice answered the phone.

"Hello! Is Mr. Fass there?"

"He's not here right now."

"Do you know where he is?"

"Who's speaking please?"

"It's his accountant, Mr. Mencher. It's very important that I reach him."

"Just a minute," and he handed the phone over to someone else.

"Is that you, Calman?" came a sweet voice over the phone. "This is Helena."

"Helena!" he was surprised and happy to hear her voice. "I haven't seen you or Emeric for quite some time. How are you and what are you doing there?"

"Gula is so busy that I am helping him out for a while. I enjoy working here. Are you looking for him?"

"Yes! I need to speak to him. It's rather urgent."

"He had a meeting with Mr. Norris, the bank manager. If it's very important you can probably reach him at the bank. I'll give you the number."

"Never mind, Helena! Please make sure he returns my call when he gets back."

"Don't worry! I'll phone you the moment he gets in the door."

Calman's phone buzzed. "Yes Audrey!

"Are you trying to reach Mr. Fass?"

"Yes! Is he on the line?"

"Line two!"

"Hello, Gula?"

"It's Helen! Just a minute, Calman!"

He heard her address someone: "Pick up the line, Gula."

"Hello! Who is this?"

"It's Calman Mencher," Calman spoke curtly. "I've just had another irate call from the tax department. Listen, Mr. Fass, we cannot continue to put them off. Do you have the information I requested?"

Fass was apologetic. "I need two, maybe three more days."

"Are you sure?"

"Yes."

"O.K. Can you bring it to my office as soon as it is compiled?"

"Yes!"

Fass did not come to Calman's office at the expiration of three or even four days. Nor did he appear by the end of the month. Nor did he phone. When Peterson called, Calman did not accept the call. Instead he got into his Pontiac and headed for European Food Imports. When he arrived he was greeted by a smiling Mrs. Stern from the reception area.

"Hello Calman. I didn't know you were coming today." She took his arm and ushered him into the office. "How is Ruth?"

"She's fine," he replied impatiently.

"And how are the little ones?"

"The little ones," he replied, "are night owls, and they keep us from getting any sleep."

"You must bring them up to our home for a visit."

She went into the warehouse to get her brother, and Calman followed. He was surprised at the extent to which the plant and warehouse had expanded. Fass came right over and they shook hands. "What do you think of our plant?" he asked proudly.

"Impressive," Calman answered him.

But Calman would not allow himself to be diverted. So he started right in: "Mr. Fass, can we talk somewhere in private?" Fass led him into his private office, which was cluttered with papers and various product samples. Calman decided on a new tactic. He would be placatory.

"Jules, please listen to me…" Gula put up a hand to stop Calman, and walked to the desk. He then opened a drawer, pulled out a sheet of paper, and proudly handed it to Calman. Calman looked at the sheet, noted several names listed and an amount opposite each name. He turned the sheet over, saw that it was blank, and reversed it again. At a glance he could see that the listed amounts did not exceed three thousand dollars in total.

He turned to Fass and gave him a look of incredulity:"What is this?"

"You wanted a list of the people to whom we sold jewelry. This is it."

An exasperated Calman started to shout. "My God, man, I'm looking for a list that totals millions of dollars. This is a pittance. You've given me six names…"

Fass corrected him calmly: "Seven…"

"Excuse me, seven."

Mrs. Stern poked her head in. "Cal, would you like some freshly brewed coffee with some strudel?"

Calman shook his head, "No, thank you Helen!"

Calman sat down in Fass's swivel chair, and motioned to Fass to sit down too. He crossed his hands over his chest, fixed his eyes on a spot on the floor, and took a long moment to collect his thoughts. Then looking directly into Fass's eyes he began to speak softly, but slowly and deliberately.

"My friend, I believe you have a very serious problem. I don't know if you realize just how serious it is. Do you understand what I am saying?" Fass shifted uncomfortably, and Calman continued. "I want to help you, not only because I am your auditor, but your friend. Do you believe me?" Fass nodded. "Good! But I can't help you if I don't know what's going on. You may feel that your personal affairs are none of my business, and you are right. But this fellow Peterson is a tenacious bulldog, and he is making your personal affairs his business. He intends to get to the bottom of the mystery. Now, if you have done nothing wrong, you have nothing to fear. Simply tell him what he wants to know, and get rid of the pest. But if there is something going on that is not 'kosher' rest assured he will pursue you and you will face prosecution.

"The penalty, if you are found guilty of tax evasion could be a heavy fine as well as a prison sentence. I hate to scare you like this, but I would be doing you a disservice if I did not forewarn you. I cannot put off the taxman any longer."

An ashen-faced Fass stood up, and shook hands with Calman:

"Thank you very much, Mr. Mencher, for coming to see me."

"Is that all you have to say to me?" Calman asked, but Fass had already gone into the warehouse.

As Calman passed the reception area on his way out Mrs. Stern greeted him again, "Are you leaving so soon, Calman?"

"Yes," he said, "I have another appointment."

CHAPTER XIII

Calman was mentally exhausted from his frustrating encounter with Fass. He looked at his watch as he got into the car and realized it was nearly four P.M., and decided to go home instead of returning to the office.

On the way home his mind was preoccupied with the question: *What shall I tell Peterson tomorrow?* He could not put him off any longer. The man was on the trail, dogging Gula, a bloodhound who would not give up, a veritable Inspector Javert. *But*, he thought, *What had Gula done? Was he being exploited by someone, an innocent dupe? Well*, Calman concluded, *I have one of two choices…either turn over the passbook to Peterson or resign. I'll discuss this with Ruth tonight. She always has sound advice.*

He arrived home, parked the car in the garage and entered the house through the side door. But he could not escape the melee. Two mites came charging at him with cries of 'daddy' and 'dada'. He bent down and enfolded them in his arms, and all the fatigue melted away. Now the three of them were down on the floor, a mass of capering, flouncing arms and legs.

"Don't hurt Daddy," came the cheerful voice from the doorway. These words were all the children needed to send them into a new frenzy of romping and savagery. At last peace returned to the household, and the children turned their attention to the black Labrador, Licorice, and Ruth and Calman were able to exchange a few words.

Calman walked into the living room and sank into an armchair. He picked up the *Telegram*, one of the dailies to which they subscribed and turned to the editorial page. But he soon put it down and closed his eyes.

Ruth, meanwhile, had taken a brandy glass from the cabinet, poured some Hennessey into it, and heated it over a flame. She handed him the glass and remarked,

"You seem troubled. Do you want to talk about it?" Calman put the glass to his lips and inhaled deeply, allowing the aroma to penetrate his nostrils, and then sipped slowly.

His eyes half-closed he muttered, "O to Dionysus, god of the spirits, let me take comfort from thy nectar; for I've had a lousy day."

"So bad, huh!" said Ruth. "Did you lose a client?"

"No, nothing like that! Do you remember the Stern and the Fass families?"

"Of course," she nodded.

"Well, I think they're in trouble…big time."

"Really? Those nice people? What could they have done?" Calman then recounted the events of the past few days.

Ruth said,

"I'm shocked. It's hard to believe they could be involved in any criminal activity. They seem to be such gentlefolk." Ruth was preparing the children's meal, "Let me feed the children. Then you can help me bathe them and put them to bed. Afterwards we'll have dinner, and we can talk about it." "O.K?

"Yes! O.K."

Ruth served dinner and joined Calman at the table. "So," she said as she placed a large bowl containing salad on the table, "it seems that there are actually two questions to be answered: First, where did the money come from and why, and second, to whom was it paid and why? Is that right?"

"Correct!"

"And the income tax people…..What do you call them?"

"The Department of National Revenue!"

"Yes! They want to know how Mr. Fass came into these funds?"

"Precisely!"

"Are you certain this is what they are looking for?"

"Ruth, they must know already that some thirty million dollars was banked and withdrawn. Why, otherwise, would they call to enquire? They will want to see a detailed statement of what we refer to as a source and application of funds."

"How would the government know about these deposits and withdrawals in the first place? Aren't bank records supposed to be confidential?"

"Hah! You're so naive. It could be anything. The bank has a duty to report unusual deposits and withdrawals. Or, it may be that they were doing an audit on someone else, and they came across a large payment to Fass which did not match up when they crosschecked it against his income. Or it may be that someone tattled on him."

"Hmm!" murmured Ruth, "it's too bad. They're such nice people. Do you think they might be involved in something illegal?"

"It's hard to believe, isn't it? They seem to be so artless, so guileless," Calman replied.

"Yes," said Ruth, "but appearances can be deceiving."

After a few moments reflection Ruth said, "Look, you are his financial adviser, right?"

"I thought I was, but obviously I'm not."

Ruth got up to serve the next course. "So wife," Calman needed a little comic relief, "what did you make for my dinner?"

"Hamburgers with mashed potatoes and onions, husband."

"What, no corned beef hash?"

"That's for dessert." They bantered for a little while.

Then Calman said reflectively:

"I keep wondering about the Sterns and the Fasses. They are honest, hard-working people of modest means, and they live modestly. Neither of the couples owns a home. The Fasses lease a house and the Sterns live in a one-bedroom apartment. So, I keep asking myself, 'how did they suddenly come into such large sums of money'?"

A light suddenly went on in Ruth's mind:

"I know! It's an inheritance!"

"If that were true," said Calman, "they would probably have received one, or, at the most, two large amounts, but these deposits are spread over three years, and they don't seem to follow any pattern. Moreover, why would they have to be so secretive?"

Ruth tried another tack: "You've told me they were once people of wealth. Maybe they were unable to get their money out of Hungary before and now they're getting it out gradually."

Calman thought for a moment, and said: "But then again, why are they so secretive about it?"

"Well," Ruth asked, "do you have any other thoughts?"

Calman said, chewing on his words: "I hate to even think it, but they might be kiting cheques."

"Kiting cheques? What does that mean?"

"It's where a dishonest businessman will issue a check on one bank, in which he does not have enough funds, and deposit it in another bank in order to raise money or sustain credit, and then issue a check back to the first bank. But sooner or later he gets caught. However, I can't see what Stern or Fass would have to gain from such shenanigans."

"What other explanations can you think of?"

"Maybe he's laundering money for someone."

"What is that?"

"This is how it works. A person is in possession of money obtained by theft, or from the sale of illicit drugs, or some other criminal offense. He wants to make these funds kosher, so he finds a patsy who has no criminal record, and gives him the money to deposit, and he pays the patsy a small percentage, maybe five or ten percent to deposit it in his personal account. Then the patsy returns the money to the source, less his cut, and attempts to make it look like a legitimate business transaction."

"I don't understand it. It seems hardly worthwhile."

"Well, you would be surprised at the number of such patsies in the world."

"Cal, do you think this is what could have happened?"

"Maybe, but this is too transparent, and Stern is not a fool.

They considered both possibilities for a while, and Ruth declared: "No! That is not possible."

"Anything is possible. At this point I wouldn't discount anything."

"But don't you see, that would be totally out of character for both of them."

"You mean it's psychologically impossible?"

"It would be quite abnormal."

"Well you would be surprised at how many honest people there are who think nothing of cheating on their income tax returns. They are otherwise perfectly honest. They would not cheat their partners, they would not cheat at poker and they would not cheat in business.

There was a case recently of a fellow who wrote off the cost of his son's Bar Mitzvah. He got caught and had to pay the tax as well as a penalty. The man was a lawyer. Do you know how he tried to explain it away? He contended that he had invited a number of his clients and colleagues to the affair, and that it should therefore be allowed as a promotion expense."

"So you believe they are not really dishonest. They are simply rationalizing away their bad judgment."

"Well Ruth, I can't say. I'm not a psychiatrist. But whatever may be their motive, I can tell you this: Peterson is not going to disappear."

"That's true." And summing up all they had discussed she added: "And they won't offer any explanation."

"Not a hint. And I find myself under a great deal of pressure because of them."

Ruth muttered: "The game is not worth the candle."

"What?"

"Oh! Nothing! It's just an expression!" They sat at the table reflecting, Calman stirring his tea indifferently.

"So what do you recommend I do?"

She did not hesitate: "I think you should call Mr. Stern this evening, before it gets too late.

"Not Mr. Fass?"

"No, Mr. Stern! You've gotten nowhere with Mr. Fass. Talk to him about your concerns, and ask him to come to your office tomorrow and to bring Mr. Fass with him."

"And what if they don't come, or what if they come but refuse to cooperate?"

"Then you have no choice but to resign. Return their passbook to them. Phone this Peterson chap and tell him you are no longer their accountant.

However, I think they will come and that they will confide in you, and who knows, there may be a totally rational explanation behind these strange happenings."

CHAPTER XIV

Ruth got up and started to clear the table. "Phone Mr. Stern now," she said.

"Let me help you first," Calman offered.

"All right, I'll wash and you dry."

They worked together quietly for a while. Ruth was having trouble returning a large platter to the top shelf of the kitchen cabinet. She stood on her toes but could not reach the shelf. Calman came up behind her, took the plate out of her hands and hemming her against the sink returned it to its place. He encircled her waist and drew her into himself. She grew soft and extended her bottom into him. He became hard as his hands sought her breasts. He pulled down the zipper of her dress and was biting into her nape when the doorbell rang. Calman let out a rare expletive, "Shit!" He went to the door while Ruth straightened out her dress and ran her hand through her hair. He opened the door and there stood four unexpected visitors. Calman was staggered.

"Well, hello! Come in, come in," he gasped.

"Who is there?" Ruth called.

"You'll never guess, dear," he responded. In a moment Mr. And Mrs. Stern and Mr. And Mrs. Fass were in the hallway, all four laden with gifts of food products—chocolates, cookies and jams.

Fass explained jovially, "We were driving in the area, and we decided to drop in on you, that is, of course, if you're not too busy."

Ruth appeared, and Helena and Malka immediately went over to embrace her. "We would love to see the children, if they're not already asleep," said Helena.

"Yes, we would love to," Malka echoed.

"Well, they've been put to bed, but I don't think they're asleep yet. They like to chat with their gremlins before they fall asleep."

"Why don't you ladies spoil my children, while we men solve the world's problems," Calman jested as he led Stern and Fass towards the den.

The den was small but comfortable. The walls were lined with oak book-shelves, stacked with books, except for a narrow indentation where a stand rested containing eight canes. A baroque oak table served as a desk. The desktop was clear except for three books neatly lined up—a dictionary, a thesaurus and a translation of Cervantes's novel *Don Quixote*. The hard-wood floor was partially covered by an oriental rug, on which rested a small rectangular wooden coffee table, at each end of which was arranged a cozy semi-circular leather chair. Calman motioned his visitors to be seated and moved his office desk chair between them.

Stern noticed the cane-stand and stepped towards it. He glanced at the canes for a moment and then deposited his own ebony cane in the stand amongst Calman's collection. A guilty notion passed through Calman's mind. "I hope he forgets to retrieve his cane when he leaves and then forgets where he left it." But that thought evaporated quickly. "No! I'll remind him to take his cane before the evening ends."

Once they were all seated Calman broke the strained silence. "Gentlemen, can I offer you a drink?" He stood up. "Let me see. I've got rye, I've got scotch I've got rum." They both declined. He was about to offer to show them his wine cellar in which he took great pride, but realized that his frivolity was forced, and he resumed his seat instead.

Surprisingly, the usually taciturn Mr. Stern now took the lead. "Mr. Mencher," Stern began, "You have been putting much pressure on my brother-in-law to explain how it happens that large sums of money have been deposited into a special bank account which we have opened up, and this is causing us much distress."

Calman intruded, "I'm not doing this because I'm a busybody, but when the tax authorities start asking questions it is best that we give them answers, and I mean truthful answers. Believe me, gentlemen, one does not play games with these people"

"We understand this, Mr. Mencher. That is why we have come here this evening. We place our trust in you, and we need your advice. But we must ask you to swear an oath that you will not reveal what we are going to tell you, even if it means you cannot talk about it to this Mr. Peters."

"Peterson," Calman corrected him. "Yes, do we have your oath?"

Calman retorted, "Gentlemen, an oath is not something to be taken lightly. If what you have to say to me can solve this dilemma, why not tell Peterson and be done with it?"

"Because, Mr. Mencher, it is not that easy. After we leave you may talk about it to your wife, in whom we also have confidence, but you must also get her promise not to disclose this to anyone. Do we have your oath?"

Calman was taken by surprise by the revelation of this new side to the character of the timid Mr. Stern. "All right," he replied, "You have my promise, but I give it reluctantly!"

"Fine," Stern continued, "I think you already know that my family once owned the most prominent jewelry business in Hungary. My grandfather started the business but it was my father who made it prosper. We catered mainly to the upper class and people of rank—earls, dukes, counts, and barons. Our customers came from Austria, Germany, even from France. Our reputation was known throughout Europe." Calman wanted to interrupt, but he did not. He began however to suspect that he was about to be subjected to a repetition of Fass's fiction about selling family jewels in Canada.

"After World War I we were very fortunate. We were spared from the starvation and the epidemics that spread across Europe, and thanks to God, my family was able to help out in the community. This, of course, Calman, was before your time. You may have read about it, but you did not experience it. The only casualty in our family was myself. I returned from the front with loss of health, constant nightmares, and lapses of memory. But I don't want to talk about that. Gula and my sister had become engaged during my absence, but they delayed their wedding until I recovered. When they got married my father gave them a one-third partnership in the business. I married Helena in 1926, and we were also given a one-third interest in the business as a wedding present."

Calman wondered, *Why is he telling me this? What does it have to do with a Canadian income tax audit in a different corner of the world thirty-three years later?* But he said nothing and permitted Stern to continue without interruption.

"Now, there was my younger brother, Joseph. I cannot explain why he had become a delinquent, or, in my father's own words, a ne'er-do-well. Perhaps it happened because of the war years; perhaps because, being the youngest, he was spoilt a bit, or maybe he resented all the attention given to me when I returned home from the war an invalid. But now that he was no longer a child he left the Academy and began to associate with the wrong people – petty thieves, gamblers and hoodlums. He did not work, but spent the money my father gave him on gambling and drinking. Sometimes he did not come home all night, and when my mother saw that his bed had not been slept in, she would cry, but would not tell my father. Joseph had become a wastrel, and it was apparent he would, sooner or later, get into trouble with the law."

There was a knock at the door, and Ruth came in carrying a tray of coffee and the cookies, which the guests had brought. She was about to say something, but observing the serious looks on their faces, she turned around and left, leaving the tray behind. Emeric and Jules drank their coffee black. Calman had his with milk and sugar and helped himself to a cookie. "My, this tastes good," Calman said, "Are they produced here or do you import them?"

Jules replied, "Every product we sell comes from Europe. There are a lot of people living here in Toronto who come from Central and Eastern Europe, and they are our biggest customers. But we don't sell directly to them. We sell mostly to the Viennese bakeries, the Hungarian restaurants and other specialty eating places, and now the department stores are taking an interest in us. We've received orders from the two major department stores, Eaton's and Simpson's, would you believe it. But I don't think we'll continue to do business with them."

"Why would you want to cut them off?" Calman asked him. "Everybody vies to get them as customers."

"Because the orders they want to place with us are too large for us to handle. Also they expect to get the products at a preferred price; plus, they want to take a two per cent discount. And, as if that were not enough they don't want us to sell to anyone else. If I do what they want I'll soon be out of business and I'll be working for them alone."

CHAPTER XV

The interlude was over, and Stern started in again. Joseph was a troubled young man, bringing home failing marks from school and associating with a gang of miscreants. His mother was worried about him, and his father had become fed up with his mischievous pranks. One day there was a knock at the door. Mama Sarah was up stairs, so she called down to Malka: "See who's at the door dear."

Malka opened the door and found a tall, heavyset young policeman, holding Joseph in a firm grip by his coat collar. "This boy says that he lives here," the policeman boomed. "Is that true?"

"Yes!" she answered meekly, "he's my brother."

"Your brother, eh! Is your father home?"

"No, sir," she replied, looking at her brother disapprovingly, "but my mother is home. I'll fetch her."

She bounded inside and up the staircase, leaving the door slightly ajar. ""Mama," she called out, "there's a policeman here with Joseph."

The officer pushed the door open and stepped into the anteroom, dragging a reluctant Joseph with him. He recognized at once that the occupants of this home were genteel and cultured. The bookcases lined with leather-bound books, the wall hangings, the Persian rugs, the aroma of baked goods that filled the air made him feel that perhaps he had been too hasty with Joseph, and he released his hold on the boy and removed his hat. He stood with head bowed before the elegant and haughty lady as she moved towards him with deliberate steps. She glanced askance at her son.

"Joseph," she spoke authoritatively, "go to your room and wait there until your father returns." She then turned to the policeman, "Yes!" she enquired disdainfully. She did not have to say anything more.

The young officer fumbled with his hat, and addressed her apologetically: "Your son was caught stealing goods in a store. He was in the company of two young thieves who are known to us, Laszlo Csaszar and Savo Halasz. Do you know these boys?"

"I have never heard of these scamps," she replied haughtily. "What do you allege my son took?"

"A knife, a pair of leather gloves, a magnifying glass, a box of cigarettes and matches, and some sweets."

"Will my son go to jail?"

"No! Since this is his first offense no charges will be brought, but your husband will have to appear at the police station tomorrow to sign for him and to make restitution."

Mr. Gall was the principal at the all-boys' school Joseph attended. He was roundly feared and despised by most of the boys and even a number of the teachers. "Gall the ghoul" was the epithet ascribed to him when the boys were out of earshot. Gall was a formidable disciplinarian, having once served in the Hungarian Cavalry, the Hussars. His height— – he towe over the school masters, his muscularity, and the curl of his lower lip served to accentuate his chilling demeanour, and when the boys saw him pacing the halls with the strap, used to punish school miscreants, tucked under his arms, they shrunk with fear.

The class master was giving a lesson in geography, when the door opened and in stepped the ominous figure of Mr. Gall. Immediately all boys rose in unison and stood at attention. He nodded to the master, who approached him deferentially. "Carry on Mr. Barna," the principal smiled as he removed the strap together with a large black-covered book from under his arm-pit and placed them on a table nearby. The boys knew that the book was a register of those boys who had been punished, and that it contained the date of the punishment, the name of the offender, the nature of the crime, and the number of switches applied.

"Boris Virag," the master called out softly, "please tell us the difference between igneous rocks and metamorphic rocks." There was dead silence. "Boris," the principal's voice shot out like a pistol, "step forward." The boy turned ashen and shuffled forward. "Well! We are waiting for your answer—igneous rocks and metamorphic rocks!" The boy was pierced by the tormentor's look. Mr. Barna was also intimidated by the ghoul, but he tried to spare the lad.

"You see, Sir, I had given the class an assignment to review the work we have been doing on rocks, but they had to prepare for an exam in history, and I'm afraid they did not have enough time….."

He was cut off by the principal. "Well, Mr. Virag, did you or did you not do your homework?"

The terrified boy knew that he had to say something. "W..w..w..well," he stammered, "I..I..I looked it over."

"Gentlemen," the Ghoul cut him short, "Mr. Virag has looked it over," he intoned sarcastically, "and are you sure you didn't overlook it?" With this unexpected injection of humor from an unlikely source, the ubiquitous tension that had pervaded the classroom abated.

The principal continued: "All right class, you may return to your seats….. all but the three hoodlums, Laszlo Csaszar, Savo Halasz and Joseph Shtern." There was a stirring as all but the three boys resumed their seats. Gall glowered at them briefly: "You three, come with me," and without another word, even to the master, Barna, he turned and strode out of the classroom, the three boys dragging behind him. They were in the corridor when the principal suddenly stopped, and turned about, and without acknowledging their existence, ordered them, "Wait here!" He returned to the classroom. The buzzing of voices immediately ceased and the entire class rose as one again, but the Ghoul waived them back to their seats. He retrieved the strap and the black book, tucked them under his armpit, and returned to the hall. The once cocky boys, now terrified, followed meekly behind the principal.

At the end of the corridor was a wide stairway. He walked with long strides toward the stairway, and then took them two at a time. The boys did not linger, even though the distance between them and the principal grew longer. He took a few more steps to a door on which was printed in bold black and gold-trim letters the word PRINCIPAL. He opened the door and stepped into the chamber, and motioned the boys to follow. Once in the room the older man shut the door firmly as the boys huddled together, quivering.

The principal's chamber was sparse. It contained a desk with dark smooth surface on which rested a single sheet of paper and a pencil with a sharpened point. Next to the desk was a much smaller table. At one corner of the room was a bin containing six leather rods. Gall selected one, swished it in the air and tested it by striking the rod against the palm of his hand. Satisfied with its resilience he turned to face the three boys. "You, Laszlo," he pointed with the rod to the eldest boy, "Come here!" The boy hesitated, but one look from Gall was sufficient, and he moved forward shrinking. "You were warned not to climb over the school fence into Mr. Szabo's yard. You disobeyed me, and you stole apples from his trees. And now I have a letter from the police commissioner about your shoplifting escapades. I will show you what we do to thieves in this school."

He grabbed Laszlo by the back of the neck and squeezing on his nape forced him forward over the table. Gall was an expert at intimidating and terrorizing young boys. It gave him a sadistic pleasure to see them squirm under his grasp. "Now, lower your breeches," he commanded. But the boy's hands were hemmed in, and he could not move. Gall increased the pressure on his neck and Laszlo started to choke. Alarmed, Gall loosened his grip, and the boy's hands were freed. Without waiting for another command the boy groped until he found the first button and he lowered his breeches. Gall placed his hands roughly on Laszlo's undershorts and tore them apart, exposing his bare buttocks.

The other two boys watched the proceedings with terror. Again Gall tightened his grip on Laszlo's nape. They heard the hiss as the whip sailed through the air and the smack as it landed on the boy's bare buttocks. Immediately a welt appeared on his bottom, followed by swelling. They heard the piercing scream as it escaped from the boy's throat. Again they saw the whip raised high; again the smack. A second welt appeared, and the scream grew into a shriek. On the third strike blood appeared on his behind, his screams had become an increasingly high-pitched howl. He tried to escape, to wriggle free, but he was held fast.

After the fourth lash, as Gall raised the whip again, the boys saw that the torture instrument was dripping blood, and they were petrified. By the end of the eighth lash the screaming had subsided and had been replaced by a sustained groan. After the tenth blow the moaning ceased, and the boy lay inert, lifeless. "All right you." The principal cracked, "I'm through with you. Get up!" But Laszlo did not hear him. The other boys watched in horror as Gall lifted up the senseless boy with one hand, dragged his lifeless body to the corner, and dumped it there in a bloody heap.

Gall now returned the whip to the bin and selected a new one. He turned his attention to the next boy. "All right, you, Savo, you are next. Come here!" The terror-stricken boy *was* paralyzed with fear, and could not move. Gall grabbed him by his jacket and dragged his already-limp form to the table. Joseph watched in horror as Gall started the procedure once more. The adrenalin was coursing through Joseph's veins. Suddenly he was aroused to action. He rushed to the door, flung it open, and ran out into the corridor, then lurched down the stairway and into the main hallway, all the while screaming, "He killed Laszlo! He killed Laszlo!"

Two of the schoolmasters happened to be walking toward the hysterical boy, and as he was passing them one of them grabbed him. Joseph tried to squirm out of his grasp, but the man held him, and then the other master grabbed him too. He said, "I know this young man. You're Joseph Shtern, aren't you?" The boy nodded. He was shaking and out of breath. Two more masters came over, and soon, a number of students surrounded the group forming a small crowd.

One of the masters addressed them. "It's all right lads, return to your classes." He turned to Joseph and spoke kindly: "All right, son, won't you tell us what happened."

"I saw him, I saw him," Joseph cried. "Who did you see?"

"Mr. Gall! He killed Laszlo." The teachers looked at one another in astonishment.

"Where did this happen?"

"In the principal's office. He's going to do the same thing to Savo."

One of the teachers said, "We better get up there right away. I think Gall may have overstepped his bounds."

He patted Joseph on the back, and said. "All right, son. You're excused. You may go home." The four masters hurried up the stairway and into the principal's office.

The first sight that greeted the teaching staff was the naked and bloody rump of the seemingly lifeless Laszlo. One of them rushed over to feel his pulse. "I can't get a pulse. We must get a doctor right away."

Another teacher addressed the principal: "All right Mr. Gall, this time you have gone too far. Release that boy at once."

Gall looked with disgust at the assemblage and returning the whipping cane to its bin slowly walked out of the room. Two of the masters walked over to Savo who lay stretched out, face down, over the table, his buttocks sore with welts. "Can you stand up, son?" one asked. The boy managed to stand, but embarrassed by his nakedness, grabbed for his breeches, only to crumble to the floor. The master lifted the boy up in his arms and carried him to the principal's desk. Then, laying him down gently on the desk, raised his breeches and buttoned them. "Try to stand, son," he said soothingly.

Joseph ran out of the school building, but was ashamed to go home. He wandered about for hours, and finally, just before midnight he arrived at the front door. His parents were waiting for him. Rodolphe Shtern gave him a frowning stare, but said not a word. Sarah sheltered him in her arms and walked him up to his room.

CHAPTER XVI

January, 1920! A year and two months had elapsed since armistice had been declared, ending the greatest war in history. Hungary had been on the losing side, and was bankrupt. There was no money to repatriate her soldiers. So it was "each man for himself" as the men started the long trek home. Some of the returning soldiers organized themselves into disciplined units. They marched together, they foraged in unison, and they survived. Others joined gangs of unruly thugs and hoodlums. Their motto was to raid, to pillage, to steal indiscriminately. Somehow many of them also found their way home eventually, but they brought with them the thieving and criminal habits they had picked up along the way.

Thus it happened that there was a rash of break-ins and looting in the environs of the Shtern home. Some of the returning soldiers had been wounded or were too weak to walk the many miles back to their homes. They were abandoned by their comrades and left to die. They died in the rains, in the freezing winter and in the heat of summer. They died from the marauding wolves and bears. They died from starvation and from disease. Only a handful managed to return home.

Laszlo Csaszar and Savo Halasz survived their punishment. Together with the younger Joseph Shtern they formed the nucleus of a gang. After the incident with Gall each of their families received notice from the school that they had been expelled. It was not long before the gang attracted other school dropouts and mavericks. Revenge against Gall was uppermost in Laszlo's mind. "I'm going to kill him," he repeated.

The more rational Joseph pleaded, "If we kill him the police will know it was us. They'll come after us, and you know what will happen."

Laszlo shouted back, "The man must die."

Savo joined in: "I've got a better idea. Let's track him at night when he's alone. We'll jump him with sticks and knives. There will be eight of us to one of him. We'll tie him up and pull down his pants. First we'll rob him. Then we'll beat his ass until he's unconscious." The boys were relishing the idea. But they never got to execute the plan. The Ghoul had disappeared. The day he exited the classroom leaving the two beaten boys with the four masters, he also left the school. He went directly home, and without greeting his wife, packed his suitcase, took their savings and left. He was seen boarding a train, and did not get off until he reached the German lines. He enlisted in the German cavalry and held the rank of captain. One day he led a hopeless charge, sabre aloft, against the canons and machine guns of a British battalion. He and his men were mowed down, and he lay dead in the mud, his body rotting, until it was discovered weeks later after the war had ended. Gall was awarded a military medal for bravery, which was sent to his widow. She spat on it and then pledged it as collateral to a pawnbroker for a loan that she never redeemed.

One evening in January 1920, it was almost 10 o'clock and the streets were pitch black, Joseph returned home from a night of boozing, brawling and vandalism. He was a strong and muscular eighteen-year-old, and he vaulted over the gate leading into the Shtern gardens. The perimeter of the garden was lined with manicured bushes, shrubs and short branches, and as Joseph started up the stairway leading into the Shtern home, he thought he saw a rustling movement among the shrubs. "Who is there?" he called out. *It's just the wind*, he thought.

He walked to the top stair, and then onto the deck leading to the massive oak doors. He took out his key, inserted it into the groove, and was about to turn it when he thought he saw a rustling coming from the shrubs again. "Who is there?" he shouted, descending the stairs two at a time. A light came on in the house and the door opened, revealing his father standing on the open deck in dressing gown. "Is that you, Joseph, coming home so late? And why are you making such a ruckus?"

"Hello, Papa! I think we've caught one of those burglars who've been breaking into the houses in our neighborhood."

"Are you sure?"

"I think he's hiding in our bushes. I'll pull him out."

The plucky young man got on his hands and knees and crawled into the shrubbery. In a moment he called out. "I've got him." "Come out you thief."

An emaciated apparition lay there caught on a branch. Joseph pulled on his arm and the figure came loose. He pulled him out of the hedge onto the grass. "Get up!" Joseph ordered, but the figure lay prone.

Sarah came to the door, "What's the commotion?"

Her husband replied, "I think Joseph has caught one of the thieves."

She looked at the form on the ground. "Are you sure he's a thief? He looks so ill. See how thin he is. She took her husband's lantern and approached the supine man. "Are you all right?" she asked him.

He tried to talk but no words came out. He reached out to her, and croaked out a word, "Mama." Emeric was home.

CHAPTER XVII

One day Joseph came home, beaten and bruised, his clothes torn, and he smelled of spirits. But before he would go to his room to clean up Papa collared him and ordered him into his private office —the *sanctum sanctorum*. No one was, allowed into that office, except Mama, when she was cleaning. Papa saw me standing there and his look told me I was to follow them.

Papa sat down in his large leather chair behind the desk. He glowered at Joseph and pointed to a chair. Joseph sat down. No words were exchanged. He merely glanced at me: "Shut the door!" I moved quickly, on tiptoe to the door and closed it quietly. His look told me I was to sit down in the other chair at the back of the room where I would not be a distraction. Papa looked long and hard at Joseph as though trying to read something in him, until his lips began to curl in disgust. But he caught himself in this gesture and stopped abruptly, and then started tapping his fingers on the table, a habit he frequently resorted to when trying to gather his thoughts. So my father and brother sat there facing each other, two unequal antagonists. When at last my father broke the silence it was with total control and calm.

"You will remain silent when I am speaking. You will not interrupt me, and you will talk only when I invite you to talk. Do you understand me?" This was more a command than a question. Joseph nodded. Then, bringing his hands together and lacing his fingers, he said, "I want to apologize to you, my son." His voice was so low we had to strain to hear him. Joseph knew better than to interrupt. He sat still. Papa paused for a few moments to let his words sink in. Then, allowing his voice to raise a couple of octaves, he continued crisply: "Yes, I want to apologize for being so careless with your upbringing, for allowing you to become a gambler, a miscreant, a bum." His voice continued to rise. "I never thought that sending you to the best academy, paying for your fencing lessons with the finest masters, and providing you with a liberal allowance would make you into such a dissolute failure. So that is why I ask for your forgiveness."

Joseph was not a fool, and the irony was not lost on him. He squirmed in his chair, and Papa continued. Now his voice returned to its normal pitch. "I am now going to correct my mistake."

"Papa, I…I" Joseph stammered, but Papa stopped him.

"I told you not to interrupt. I have given much thought to this, and I am going to offer you a proposition. Here it is. Come into the family business…now! You are smart and it will not take you long to learn the trade. We'll find you a lovely girl. There is that nice girl, Irena Farkas, whose father is a lawyer; there is Lydia, the girl you took to the school dance. Both are pretty. And there are others. Your brother and your sister already each own a one-third share in the business. On the day you get married I will make you a gift of the remaining share."

Joseph dared to interrupt: "And what will become of you, Papa?"

He smiled for the first time: "My children will look after me…and if they don't, God will."

Joseph slumped in his chair looking down at the floor. He could not look Papa in the eyes. Papa waited for a word, a sign from Joseph. But Joseph kept a glum silence.

A few moments passed, but it seemed like hours. "All right!" Papa said, breaking the stillness again, but this time in a more cheerful tone. "Here is a second proposition. Return to the gymnasium and complete the final year, which you failed. Then, go on to the university. Study law, or medicine, or engineering or anything else worthwhile. This will take a few years. During this period you will have the encouragement and financial support of the family. If you should get married, I will make sure that all your personal financial needs, and those of your wife, are taken care of until you graduate."

There followed a wave of silence. Now, Joseph slumped in his chair, chin resting on his chest. Finally, Papa broke the silence crisply. "I give you permission to speak. What is your reply?" Again, silence. "Is there something else you would like to do?" Silence! "Do you have any plan for the future?" And now the silence seemed to take over and was doing all the talking.

Papa's voice broke into the loudness of the silence. This time his voice tone was crisp and final. "There is yet another choice you can make. You can return to your dissolute ways, your promiscuous life, and your contemptible friends. Go to your cheap bars and evil haunts. But, if you do so you shall also leave my house and never come back. I shall cut off all the financial support you have enjoyed until now, and I shall disinherit you." He stood up, and in a firm and decisive voice, he said, "Choose!" and strode out of the room.

That night, as Mama and Papa were retiring, Mama spoke to him about Joseph. "I know you had a talk with our youngest," she said, "and I can guess what happened. I spoke to him myself, but could not get a word out of him. But I do know this: Our son is very troubled. He needs our help, not our censure. I am very worried about the boy."

"But what can I do?" asked Papa, "I've made him very generous offers. Tell me what to do."

"I think," Mama answered, "that he needs time to reflect, and a place to do it, a place away from home, but also away from the bad influence of his companions."

"And just where do you think we should send our spendthrift wastrel?"

"Please Rudy, I know he has made you very angry, but thinking about him that way does not solve anything."

"I know you have already decided what to do, so tell me your suggestion."

"Let us send him on a holiday to Rome. It is a great historical city and cultural center. Joseph is sensitive, and the wonderful art and architecture and the other sights the city has to offer will inspire him. I hope he will come back to us a renewed person."

A few days later Papa called me aside and told me that Joseph was going to Rome for a holiday. He asked me to accompany Joseph to the train station, to purchase the return fare for him, and to see to it that he was safely settled in his seat on the train going to Rome.

CHAPTER XVIII

The year was 1923 when young Joseph Shtern, just turned nineteen, set off on a train from Budapest to Rome. This was the first time he had been on a train by himself. In the past his train adventures had consisted of short excursions in the company of his parents. Now, alone by himself, after the seismic confrontation with his father, he felt abandoned and wretched. He did not know what to expect when he reached his destination. He had some money with him, but not too much, so he would have to be careful how he spent it. His sister had given him a book to read, but he could not put his mind to it. A cloud of apathy descended on him, and thoughts of self-destruction began to invade his consciousness. His mind thus occupied he was abruptly roused from his thoughts by the hum of many voices.

Looking up he saw a group of young women entering the car, chattering excitedly. He counted eight of them. They were all dressed in dark-colored loose-fitting frocks that covered their necks and descended to their shoes. Each wore a white veil affixed to a large comb, which was pinned to her hair at the back of the head. Joseph surmised that they were nuns-in-training. Now, entering the car behind the young women were two older women, sisters of some order, in full nun regalia. Again, Joseph surmised, they must be the chaperones. He observed these ladies as they took their seats, and once they were settled in, he returned inward to his melancholia.

The train's whistle blew, and Joseph was once more shaken from his dolorous reflections. He looked out the window and saw the steam rise from the engines and heard the hissing sound as it escaped the compressor. Slowly the train began to move forward. But even as the train was starting nine young men, in their teens or early twenties, entered the car in pairs and took up seats. They all had short haircuts and were well groomed. They wore black suits, white shirts and black ties. None bore any jewelry, and unlike the girls who had entered a few minutes before, they spoke only in whispers. Behind them walked two priests. Their garb consisted of a brown robe made of a rough material, held together by a rope-like waistband. A hood of the same course material covered their heads, and, except for the sandals they wore, their feet were bare.

The train started to gather speed and as it got farther away from Budapest Joseph's depression began to leave him. First he watched the changing scenery, then he read his book for a while, and then he began to observe the young pilgrims across the aisle. After some time he noticed that they began opening the satchels each had carried on board, and began removing the lunches that had been packed for them. They cleansed their hands with a damp cloth, recited a short prayer and made the sign of the cross before plunging into their meals. Joseph had lost his appetite and had been unable to eat. But now, watching these novices he suddenly realized that he too was hungry. The train kept on rolling stopping only for short intervals to let passengers on and off. After a few hours of travel it arrived at Vienna. The stop here would be nearly an hour to allow a change of conductors and give the passengers a chance to stretch their legs.

The train started to roll again and Joseph returned to his seat. He felt more relaxed and closed his eyes for a few moments, only to be awakened by the feeling of someone standing over him. Alerted, he looked up to find one of the priests standing next to the seat he occupied.

"I noticed that the seat next to you is vacant. Do you mind if I take it?" Joseph shrugged and moved further away from the center, crowding himself into the corner, although there was more than ample room for both of them. The celibate sat down and making himself comfortable, addressed Joseph. "My name is Thomas, or Father Thomas as I am generally called. I am a priest, or more precisely, a Capuchin monk of the order of Saint Francis. And you are?"

Joseph was somewhat overwhelmed by this imposing yet benign figure. But he managed to muster up some courage, even a little arrogance: "And I am a Jew and my name is Joseph."

"Aha," replied the monk, "I, too, am a Jew. We who follow the ways of the Jew, Christ, whom we believe to be the Son of God, are all Jews."

Joseph was astonished to hear the priest speak in this manner. In all his previous encounters with Christian clergy he had found himself the butt of disparaging jokes. He now found himself speechless. Then, in self-defense he blurted out: "My uncle is one of the senior rabbis of Hungary."

"Yes?" said the priest, "and what is his name?"

"Avrum... Avrum Shtern."

"Avrum," repeated the priest, "that would be Abraham. Yes, Abraham and Joseph are great biblical names. Tell me Joseph...You don't mind if I call you Joseph?" The young Jew nodded. "You, of course, know who Abraham was? He was the progenitor of the Hebrews, the great Patriarch. And Joseph, as I am sure you know, since you are his namesake, was the youngest and most favored son of Jacob and Rachel to whom his father gave a coat of many colors. His jealous brothers, however, sold him into slavery, but years later, when he became a famous and powerful ruler, he forgave them all and spared them." Joseph nodded. He knew the story. "Are you learned in Talmud?"

"No sir. I only know a few words of Hebrew, but I cannot read nor converse in it."

"Now you see I am very much a Jew because I have studied Talmud," said the Capuchin monk, "and I am fluent in Hebrew."

Joseph was surprised and a little disquieted at this intelligence. He wanted to change the subject. Glancing across the aisle he asked: "Who are these young people you are accompanying?"

The priest answered him: "The gentlemen are priests in training. They are seminarians from my diocese. And the young women are novice nuns from our same order."

Joseph was drawn to this man but a little bewildered, and he needed a few moments to integrate this new experience into his consciousness. However, his thoughts again were interrupted.

"And where is your journey taking you, my son?" asked the priest. There! The relationship between them had changed. Joseph perceived at once that they were not equals any longer. They never had been. The words "My son" placed him now in a subservient position. But somehow he felt comfortable in this discipular role.

"I'm on my way to Rome, Sir," he said.

"On your way to Rome?" the monk echoed aloud. His heightened voice caught the attention of the others across the way and they began to eye the pair. "This must be the work of Providence, for we are all on our way to Rome. Tell me, what is it that brings a young Jew to Rome by himself?"

"My family hopes that in Rome I will find myself."

The priest mused about the poet, Robert Browning's Paracelsus: "I go to prove my soul." Then, with exuberance he exclaimed, "You must not, and you shall not be traveling alone. Come, I will introduce you to these novitiates, who are about your own age, and you shall complete this trip in our company.

CHAPTER XIX

By the time the train reached Rome Joseph had begun to mingle with the seminarians. Some of them had never met a Jew before and were surprised to find him so much like them. Once in Rome, each of the groups went directly to its assigned youth hostel. Father Thomas registered Joseph into a room at the same hostel where he and the seminarians were staying.

During the two weeks he spent in Rome Joseph was so preoccupied with learning about the great city and seeing its sights that he had no time to sulk over his father's severe admonition. The city of Rome, he was to learn, was not only the capital of Italy but also the locale of the Holy See. Joseph had heard of the pope before his journey, but thought of him only as a high-ranking priest. Now he discovered that the pope was in fact the head of the Roman Catholic Church, the 'Vicar of Christ'. The pope, he also learned, resided at the Vatican City which was a sovereign state within the city of Rome, a place that he would visit before his vacation ended. The history of Rome also made a great imprint on his mind. It had evolved, he discovered, from the Etruscan civilization, starting as an insignificant pastoral settlement about 800 B.C. and had expanded into the greatest cultural, intellectual and religious center of the world. It housed the world's greatest art, and was the symbol of European civilization.

On the first day after their arrival the two groups visited the Coliseum, the great Amphitheatre of Rome. Joseph stood close to the two monks, spellbound as they narrated the tales of gladiatorial combats that had once been held in this Forum. He recalled having heard or read that Titus had built it in the year 80 B.C., and to show the others that he too had some smattering knowledge of history, he asked The Fathers if that were not true.

"Partially," replied Father Thomas, smiling at him in acknowledgment, "It was actually commenced by Vespasian and completed by his son, Titus." Each day brought a new adventure into history, art or religion. On Sunday the two groups descended onto one of the great Gothic cathedrals to pray. Joseph was excused from this visit, but he insisted on staying with the group. The grandiose mass of the edifice and its lofty towers, and the sonorous resonance as the Bishop spoke from the pulpit left the Jewish youth in awe.

The best, however, was left for the last. The Sistine Chapel is the glory of the Vatican. Although not as remarkable for its architecture as some of the other edifices in the City, its fame comes from its adornments. The vari-colored marble mosaics that cover the floors, the gold sculptures, masks, candelabras and artifacts that line the great halls, and the collection of illustrated music manuscripts are bewildering. But its renown, its unique-ness, its gravitational pull for millions of people, is its wall and ceiling decorations. Frescoes by Perugino, Botticelli and other fifteenth-century artists decorate the sidewalls, depicting scenes from the lives of Moses and Christ. On the ceiling is the divine painting of Michelangelo representing the stages of creation, man's temptation and fall, Noah and the Deluge. The last great work, painted on the altar wall, also by Michelangelo, is the magnificent *Last Judgment*.

Joseph was afire by what he had just experienced. He could have burst with joy. His head was spinning and he felt as if he were being lifted and swept away by unseen wings. He withdrew from the group to gather his thoughts and recover some presence of mind. However, one of the young men, Peter, with whom he had spent more time than the others, came to fetch him.

"Joseph," he said in just more than a whisper, "I've come to get you. We're going to meet the pope."

"What!" he exclaimed, "I can't do that"

"Yes, you can, and you shall."

"But when...and where?"

"Now and here." "Here?"

"Yes! You see, the Sistine Chapel is also the private chapel of the pope in Rome."

The boys were lined up along a wall facing the altar. At each end was one of the monks. The girls were lined up in front of them with a sister at each end. They waited in silence, expectantly. Joseph ran his fingers through his hair and checked his fingernails. He was trembling. A side door opened and a white robe puffed through the room followed by some other robed figures. Afterwards Joseph could not recall the pope's features.

His neighbor whispered to him: "Pius XI."

The pope advanced down the line like a general inspecting his troops. He did not speak but wore a benign smile, and blessed each with the sign of the cross.

When he came to Joseph, the boy colored, and then with an uncontrollable urge whispered,

"I am a Jew." The Holy Father heard, but his demeanor did not change. "Then you shall be blessed twice," and he performed the rite of the cross twice and was gone.

On the train returning to Budapest Joseph mingled freely with the seminarians. But on the last leg of the journey Father Thomas sat with him.

The priest asked him,

"Well, my son, did you discover yourself in Rome?"

"I think I did, Father," he replied. "I think I should like to become an artist, and I should like to live in Rome."

"Were you inspired by the paintings of Michelangelo?"

"Yes. Very much so, and also with Da Vinci."

The priest continued, "How well are you acquainted with the Jewish bible?"

"As a young boy I was sent regularly to the 'chaider'. Do you know what that is?" The priest nodded. "I also prepared for my Bar Mitzvah."

The priest nodded again.

"Do you know the second commandment?"

Joseph thought for a minute. "I get a little mixed up with them," he fumbled.

"I understand," Father Thomas offered, sensitive to the young man's hesitation. "'You shall have no other gods beside me. You shall not make for yourself a sculptured image.' Think of that before you decide to become an artist. May I offer an opinion, my son?"

"Oh, yes! I should very much value your advice."

"Then take up your father's offer to continue your studies. For the time being take up the liberal arts, and as Plato advocated, acquire a background of knowledge in the arts and humanities before embarking on a career."

CHAPTER XX

A new and refreshed Joseph returned home. Mama and I were waiting to greet him as the train pulled in to the Budapest station. We watched as a group of novice nuns filed down the stairs onto the platform. Then we saw a group of novice priests descending, accompanied by two monks wearing brown cloaks and a hood. Suddenly, I caught a glimpse of Joseph among the priests. I caught Mama's arm:

"There he is, Mama." Now Mama saw him too and we both began to wave. Once on the platform Joseph shook hands with one of the monks and they exchanged a few words. He then waved at the others and started moving towards the gate when he caught sight of us. He strode towards us and embraced Mama and kissed her on the cheek, and shook my hand.

"Well," I asked him, "did you have a good time?" "It was the best experience of my life," he answered almost out of breath.

I recognized at once that Joseph was a new person. He had filled out a little. He was not so bony. But, most important, he had matured. He was a man. And I was a little envious. "Who were the *gollichs* you were with?" Mama asked him warily. "You mean the priests?" he said matter-of-factly, "They were some friends I met on the trip." I grabbed Joseph's luggage, and Mama took his arm. "You know, Joseph," she cooed, she was so glad to have him back home, "you don't need friends like that. And promise me something – you won't tell Papa about these goyim."

The family was waiting to greet Joseph with a million questions, and he became animated when he spoke of his Roman adventure. Helena asked him,

"Did you see the coliseum?" Joseph affected a British Oxonian accent and in exaggerated accent replied: "By any chance, Madame, might you be making reference to the Flavian Amphitheatre?" Everybody laughed, including Papa. Mama gave Papa a glowing smile. Joseph had come home. Gula wanted to know all about the Sistine Chapel. "It is ornamented with gold frescoes and statues. There must be more gold in that one edifice than in the rest of Italy." "Think if we could buy some of that gold and melt it down. We could make thousands of rings and other jewelry." Malka nudged him good humoredly: "Gula, now stop acting silly."

After a while the conversation ran out, and Joseph's mood became more pensive. Mama said: "You'll have lots of time to ask Joseph questions about his trip. In the meantime I think Joseph must be tired from his long trip. Joseph, why don't you go upstairs to your room I know you'll want to unpack, and have a good night's sleep."

During the first few days after his return Joseph spent much of his time in his room. Papa asked Mama, "What does he do in his room? Does he sit there and sulk?" "Don't be so hard on him. He doesn't sulk," she replied, "He's thinking what he wants to do with his life. It's a very important decision for him." "He should have made up his mind by now. That's why I sent him to Rome. I'm going to speak to him about it tomorrow."

Papa beckoned Joseph to follow him into his study. I was standing nearby, and Papa addressed me: "Well, are you going to join us?" I followed them into the room. They took seats facing each other, and I sat down on a couch at the back of the room, out of the line of fire.

"My son," Papa commenced, and as an afterthought, "wait here a moment." "My son," Joseph mused, and his thoughts went back to the time Father Thomas had called him that, and a good feeling entered into his soul. Papa had gone to his desk, pulled open a drawer and withdrew a bottle of brandy and three little glasses. He returned to his seat and poured three glasses of the bottle's contents. He gesticulated to me, meaning I was to take one of the glasses. He handed another glass to Joseph, and took the third for himself. I knew that I was watching a master negotiator at work. "This," he said, is to celebrate the return of my prodigal son. This brandy I save only for special occasions. It is made from the fermented juices of plums." And with that he downed his drink in one gulp. Joseph, watching his father, did the same. I sipped at mine slowly, and returned to my seat. We waited patiently as papa corked the bottle and returned it to the desk drawer. The older man...I suddenly realized that Papa looked old... returned to his seat, smacked his lips, clasped his hands, and started.

"Joseph, it appears to me that you have changed in the past two weeks. You seem to have matured. And I am very pleased for that." After a short silence, while Joseph weighed his words, he replied:

"Father, it is true. I have changed." Both men felt the divide the moment the word 'father' passed the son's lips instead of the sheltered 'papa'. Father Thomas was again brought back to Joseph's mind. "I would like to accept your proposition to return to the gymnasium and finish my studies there."

"Good, if that is your choice then I am satisfied." "And then what would you like to do?" "I am not sure." "Well," Papa interjected, "there are only a few choices available – there is the law. It would be nice to have a lawyer in the family. There is also medicine, an excellent profession. We could use a doctor in the family. Your brother had been planning to study engineering. Perhaps you would like to finish what he started. Or is there something else?" Joseph hesitated, and a silence ensued. Papa was patient.

"I am thinking of the rabbinate," Joseph offered testily. But the words exploded around us. The old man was jarred.

"What did you say? You want to be a rabbi?"

"I'm only thinking about it."

"Thinking! Thinking! Stop with this thinking. No! You will not be a rabbi," father shouted.

"What is wrong with that? Uncle Avrum is a rabbi. It's a highly respected profession," Joseph countered.

"Yes he is a rabbi, and it is a respectable profession. But Uncle Avrum started as a boy. Did you know that on the day of his Bar Mitzvah he made a speech in which he announced that he would be a rabbi, and from that day on his life was devoted to Jewish learning as well as to Jewish teaching. But you! You are twenty-seven years old. You have no Jewish learning. You never go near a synagogue. You wander around with *shegutzim* and *ganiffs*. And, even if you were serious you would have to start from the very beginning, with the *alef betz*. You would be going to a Yeshiva with twelve-year-old boys. No! No, you will not be a rabbi. I forbid it!"

"Papa," Joseph replied evenly and thoughtfully, and with no trace of anger or rebellion in his voice: "Suppose Uncle Avrum gives me his approval. What would you say then?"

"I would say that he is as mad as you."

"Notwithstanding that, if he were to give his consent to my being admitted for studies for the rabbinate, would you give your consent?"

Papa thought for a minute and then said cynically:

"Yes! Then, and only then, will you get my consent."

CHAPTER XXI

The rabbi's study was lined with books, mostly in Hungarian and Hebrew, and a few in German, English and French. There were several books and some magazines on the desk, others were piled on chairs, and a few were scattered on the floor. One had to tread carefully to avoid stumbling over the books. The rabbi ushered his nephew into the room and lifted a tower of books from one of the chairs and placed them on the floor. He motioned to Joseph to be seated. The rabbi's wife, the *rebbitzin*, entered carrying a tray of strudel.

"Please Hannah," the rabbi said, "we do not want to be disturbed." The strudel consisted of a very light thin crisp dough filled with Turkish delight, nuts and honey. She placed the tray on the desk in front of Joseph. "I want Yosele to sample his favorite pastry. I won't trouble you anymore," and she left closing the door behind her.

The rabbi sat down and started fumbling on the desk, looking for his spectacles. He lifted several books and magazines but could not find what he was looking for. "When that woman cleans this room, which I beg her not to, I can never find anything again," he groaned.

Joseph held up a pair of glasses, which he retrieved from under a small heap of paper. "Is this what you're looking for, Uncle," he asked. "Yes," he replied, accepting the glasses and adjusting them on his nose. The rabbi now sat back in his chair, stroked his beard, smacked his hands and then started rubbing them together as though he were washing them. He was ready for business.

"So Yosele, my spies tell me you went on a trip to Rome? Is that so?" He did not wait for an answer. "It would have been better if you had gone to Jerusalem." Joseph did not reply, but waited for the Elder to signal him to speak. "So," continued the rabbi, "What is so important you had to see the elder rabbi right away?"

"Did papa speak to you?"

"No, and he should be ashamed he never calls his older brother." Joseph recounted his experiences on his way to Rome and in Rome. The older man listened attentively. When he was through the old man asked, "And you actually spoke to the pope and told him that you are a Jew?" Joseph nodded. "And he blessed you twice?"

"Twice," Joseph repeated. The chimes of the grandfather clock in the parlor struck six, and Rebecca opened the door again.

"You'll stay for dinner Yojikam?" "No, tante," Joseph replied, "I am expected home." Her husband gave her a look of impatience and the kindly woman closed the door and returned to the kitchen. "I don't think you came here especially to tell me you met this *gollich* – this, this monk."

"No, Uncle! I came because I am having a big argument with my father, and I need your help."

"There's nothing unusual about that," the rabbi observed, "young men are always pitting themselves against their fathers. So, what is this great quarrel about that you need an arbitrator?" Joseph took a deep breath.

"My father wants me to join him and Emerich in the jewelry business or to enter a profession, such as medicine, or law, or engineering, one that he thinks will bring the family prestige, but he rejects outright my own feelings in this respect."

"I see," said the uncle. "This is not uncommon. I see this problem all the time. Young boys always rebel against their fathers. Do you know why? Because they have to prove themselves!" Joseph thought of Father Thomas' words from Browning's Paracelsus, "I go to prove myself." But they usually come back to their good senses, as I know you will."

"No, Uncle Avrum, I think I am beyond the proving stage."

"Precisely! You are a man, and should not need to rebel anymore."

"That is just the point. I am a man, and I know what I want. But my father is adamantly opposed to what I want to do?"

"I have known your father his entire life. Believe me, he's a good man, and he is smart. I don't think he is looking for prestige for himself or the family. And I am sure he is only interested in what is best for you. The opportunity he is offering you would provide you with status in the community and security. Don't you agree?"

"Yes, I know my father is a good man and that he is looking out for my best interests."

"So, there you are, it's all set..."

Joseph interrupted: ""My father THINKS he is looking out for my best interest, but he does not know me."

"Know you?" the rabbi was dumbfounded.

"Understand me!" Joseph corrected himself.

"All right, he does not understand you. So tell me, what is it then that you would like to do?" Joseph took a deep breath:

"I want to become a rabbi," the young man blurted out.

The old man's left cheek began to twitch. "What? I didn't hear you."

Joseph repeated his words very succinctly: "I want to become a rabbi."

Rabbi Shtern stood up slowly and excused himself. "You will have to excuse an old man. It becomes more difficult to hold one's water as one gets older. Wait here." And he walked shakily towards the door.

Ten minutes later the rabbi was seated in his chair again. Now he was all business. "Did I understand you to say you want to become a rabbi?" Joseph nodded. "Tell me Joseph, how old are you?"

"I'm almost thirty."

"Almost thirty," the rabbi repeated with a twinge of irony. "Have you studied Torah?"

"No."

"No," the rabbi imitated him. Then again: "Have you studied Gamara?"

"No."

"No," he kept mimicking Joseph for emphasis. "Have you studied Mishna? Do you know anything about the Talmud?" Joseph did not answer. "Who was Rabbi Akiva? He was a great Hebrew scholar. Who was the Goan of Vilna? Ach! I take that back. How would you know? But every chaider boy knows this: Who was Musa ibn Maimon, the Rambam? You do not know. All right: Who was Spinoza?"

Joseph jumped in: "He was a Jewish philosopher."

"Wrong! He was excommunicated from the Jewish community for blasphemy. Tell me, who was Moses Mendelssohn? You have never heard of him or any of these people. Am I right?" Joseph did not answer. "Do you know anything about the history of the Jewish people?" the rabbi asked wryly. "All right! Can you speak, read or write a single word of the Hebrew language? The answer is no, no, and again, no."

Throughout this diatribe Joseph remained mute. Then the rabbi continued in a more kindly vein. "My dear nephew, I don't mean to discourage you, but to challenge you so that you may see how foolhardy your plan is. Can you imagine yourself, a man of thirty, studying at a Yeshiva with a group of twelve-year-old boys? Give up this '*michegaus*', this insanity." Joseph sat mute before the patriarch, and then thought of one final ploy to persuade him.

"Uncle, I know that you have wanted your own son, Herchel, to follow your profession. But he has no interest in becoming a rabbi." The rabbi nodded. "So he's going into the profession he loves, architecture. Isn't that right?"

"Yes, that is right." Joseph felt encouraged.

"Now, you would rather he became a rabbi, but he wants to do something else with his life. He respects your wishes, but he must write his own existence. I am the only member of our small family that wants to enter the profession of the rabbinate, and to keep alive the tradition you carried on from your father, my grandfather of blessed memory. I admit I have wasted a few years, but I have changed, and I am still young, am willing to study hard. If I succeed it will be an honor to you that I will be continuing your work. And if I fail I will know soon enough and can then go into my father's jewelry business."

"Are you finished?" the rabbi asked him. Joseph nodded expectantly. "First of all, I congratulate you. I did not know you could argue so eloquently. You have just proved to me that you would make a great lawyer. Secondly, don't call the rabbinate a profession. Architecture, engineering, law are professions. If you wanted to switch from one profession to another I say good luck. But the rabbinate is not a profession or a vocation. It is a calling, a mission. You have to be born with it. You, my son...he was beginning to sound like Father Thomas... are simply going through a phase. It will pass. But, in the meantime, if you are unable to decide what to do with your life, return to study for a year. I can assure you that by that time you will have come to your senses."

"So, you think I have no chance?" the crestfallen Joseph asked his uncle.

"Why do you make it sound like a loss? Of course there's always a chance," the rabbi replied, "but when I consider your ignorance about Judaism at your age, and your course of conduct during the last few years, not to mention the kind of friends with whom you hang out, I must tell you that you have very little chance of being accepted into the Hebrew College for Rabbinical Studies."

"What would happen if I applied?"

"Don't!" the rabbi ejaculated. "As you know I sit on the board of the college, and I have to tell you candidly that I will cast my vote against admitting you. I could not, in good conscience, recommend you for rabbinical studies. So take my advice. Don't shame the family. Save yourself the embarrassment of rejection. I repeat what I have already said—if you cannot settle on a lifetime vocation now, then return to the gymnasium, complete your studies over there, and then make up your mind."

CHAPTER XXII

Joseph returned to a tense home. He was late for the evening meal, but Mama refused to serve the meal until her youngest son had returned. The moment he walked through the doorway, Malka called out: "He's here! At last we can eat.

No one ventured to speak to him except Mama. "So tell us Yosele did you see Uncle Avrum?"

"Yes!"

"And what did he have to say?"

"He said No!"

Father pounded his fist on the table. "Let that be the final word. That subject is from now on forbidden in this house." Without another word Joseph stood up and left the table, and ascended the stairs to his room.

"Yosele, you'll come down soon for dinner?"

"No, Mama! I'm not very hungry."

"I think he's upset," she said to Papa.

"He'll get over it."

Joseph returned to the gymnasium, but came home every evening for dinner with the family, after which he would retire to his room to read and study. Papa observed on the remarkable change that had come over his youngest son during the past few months. One evening papa was sitting in the living room reading his newspaper and mama was also there knitting. Papa put down his paper and remarked to her,

"Now he's too quiet." But Mama warned him with her woman's intuition: "You know Rodolfe, a too drastic change is sometimes not so good. Let him alone. I think he's going through some kind of mental upheaval. Time will cure whatever is ailing him."

"I don't know. I don't understand him. He seems to be completely estranged from the family. Have I been such a bad father? Tell me what I have done wrong?" "No," she said, "I don't think it has anything to do with you." Papa picked up the paper again.

"Sarah, have you ever heard of a Dr. Sigmund Freud? There is an interesting article about him in the papers," he said, handing her the papers. "He treats people with mental disorders. Maybe our Yosele needs a little hypnosis or analysis to wake him up."

"Please don't speak like that. Our son is not crazy," she cried.

"I didn't say that Yosele is crazy. But how do we know," he came back, "we have never had anything like this in the family before. I think I will write to this Dr. Freud."

"No, I beg you, please don't," she sobbed. "He's not crazy."

Joseph had given up his rowdy ways and had become a serious student. His marks kept improving. He had also taken up the habit of taking long walks by himself. On one such occasion his meandering brought him to the doorstep of a building that housed the seminarians of the Order of Saint Francis. He approached the door, which was heavy, oaken and imposing. He also took note of the garden, which was elegantly landscaped, and he saw two monks pruning the bushes. One of them noticed Joseph noticing them, and approached him smiling:

"Are you looking for someone?"

Although it was quite by accident that Joseph had arrived at the seminary, he replied without faltering: "I am looking for Father Thomas."

There was a long hallway indented by doors leading to the monks' bare quarters, which contained only a cot, a single chair, a small wooden table, a wash basin and a lamp. In the sparse hallway, with low ceilings and dim lights, there was a snug alcove where a visitor could be greeted. This was the nook to which Joseph was led and where he was greeted by Father Thomas. "Hello Joseph, it is good to see you again," the monk welcomed him. "I regret I can offer you very little, for, as you see, we live a very simple life here."

"Your hospitality is more than I could ask for," replied the guest. There was a pause in the conversation before the priest started. "So Joseph have you completed your studies at the gymnasium yet?"

"Yes! I completed my final exams last month."

"And when do you commence your rabbinical studies?"

"I'm afraid I will not become a rabbi. You see my father is opposed to my entering the clergy. He does not think I have the moral character for that vocation. And my uncle, who is an ordained rabbi and the chair of the admissions committee at the rabbinical college is also opposed to my admission. He thinks I am too old to enter the rabbinate, and that I lack the proper moral attitude and the requisite background in Hebrew studies. He has informed me that he will oppose my admission."

"I'm sure your uncle is a wise man. Do you not find some merit in his reasons?"

"I think that both he and my father believe that I will bring shame to the family."

"And will you?"

Joseph stood up. "I'm afraid I have to leave now. Thank you, Father Thomas, for allowing me to visit with you." The priest also stood up: "I will walk you to the entrance." As they walked along the narrow corridor the monk remarked: "I'm sorry I've not been of much help to you, my young friend, but let me make a suggestion to you. Why not enroll in a course on philosophy? This could lead to a professorship, which is as close as you can come to being a rabbinical scholar, for as I understand it, rabbi means teacher." They shook hands, and Joseph turned and was gone.

CHAPTER XXIII

The family was seated around the dinner table. The usual interchange of opinions was lagging, and so Papa introduced a topic. "What do you think about this fellow in Germany and his national socialist party?"

"Oh," Gula spoke up, "You mean this clown Hitler?" "Yes." Helena said, I've been reading about him, and you know what? He'll never defeat Hindenburg in an election. Besides, he won't last—here today, gone tomorrow—he's a nothing. Just a windbag."

Mama interjected with her usual logic: "And he's in Germany. We're in Hungary. What does he have to do with us here?"

Papa looked across the table where Joseph was seated: "And what does our latest graduate say?"

"Wellll," Joseph elongated the word, "he's a virulent Jew-hater and the depression is bringing him new followers every day. His anti-Semitism has already spread to Austria, and has begun to spread to Hungary. I think he's very dangerous, and we can't afford to be too casual about him." The table fell silent, not only because this was the longest utterance Joseph had made in a year, but because of its sobriety.

It was finally broken by Papa: "Thus spoke our prophet of doom." "Besides," Gula added, "During the first World War he was a lance corporal. How can he possibly shoot up to the position of head of state, the chancellor of Germany?" There followed a little small talk, until Papa finally broke it up.

"Tell us Joseph," he looked into the eyes of his youngest son, "now that you have graduated from the gymnasium, what are your plans?" Joseph stared directly into his father's eyes unwavering, in return, and then almost insolently:

"I would still like to enter the rabbinate." His father cut him off at once.

"Don't trifle with me. This matter was settled last year."

"All right," Joseph responded evenly, "I want to study philosophy."

"Philosophy?" the old man blared. "Did you ever hear such idiocy? He wants to become a philosophe! What kind of living will you make from this profession Mr. Socrates?"

"I will teach."

"And where will you teach."

"At the university!"

"At the university? What university will give a Jew a teaching post? You would be lucky if they let you sweep the floors. What is wrong with becoming a lawyer or a physician or an engineer?"

"Those professions are all right for certain people, but they are not of any interest to me." "The old man blared again in anger: "I gave you a number of alternatives. The time has now come to make a choice…CHOOSE!"

Joseph said nothing, but stood up, set his folded napkin on the table, made a slight bow to his father, turned around and left. Mama called after him: "Yojikam, you didn't eat your dessert."

Joseph walked for several hours and finally, in the late afternoon he arrived at a park and sat down on a bench to rest. He was weary and closed his eyes. Soon he fell asleep and started to dream, only to be awakened by someone touching him. He opened his eyes to confront an aged man shaking him.

"I'm sorry to disturb you," said the stranger, "but it seemed to me that you were going to fall off the bench. Are you all right?" Joseph nodded and sat upright, allowing the stranger room to sit down beside him. The old man took the seat and started to hum. Joseph began to observe him and saw that he was very thin, and seemed to be ailing. The old man's face contained a long nose that came to a point and a chin that also came to a point, and piercing eyes. His clothes were in tatters. He was obviously very poor, perhaps a beggar. Yet he appeared to be content, happy with the lot fate had dished out to him. This caricature was carrying a brown paper bag, which Joseph had not noticed previously, and from which he extracted a sandwich, and proceeded to offer half of it to Joseph. Joseph surprised himself by accepting the man's offering and downing it like a famished wolf. Then the old man did something bewildering. He put his hand back in the bag and withdrew a tallith – the Jewish prayer shawl, kissed it, and placed around his shoulders. He turned to the East and began to 'daven', to recite the early evening prayer, bending and bowing and chanting. When he had finished praying he returned the tallith to the bag, stood up and made the sign of the cross. As he left he said to his astonished companion:

"Joseph, tonight your destiny will be settled."

The young man called after him: "Say, how did you know that my name was Joseph?" but he had disappeared into the mist.

CHAPTER XXIV

Joseph sat on the bench for some time, deep in thought, reflecting on this strange, enigmatic visitor. "What mysterious forces had brought him to my side? What is the meaning of the mixing of the Jewish prayer with the sign of the cross?" For more than an hour he sat thus transfixed, when he was awakened by a burst of thunder. The sun had already set and night had fallen.

Half an hour later, Joseph found himself once more at the door of the monastery. He looked around to see if there was anyone about. But not a soul was to be seen. He knocked at the massive door but no one answered. Then he noticed a bell and he started pulling the rope, which set off a gong. Almost immediately the door opened, and a young man dressed in monk's garb appeared. Joseph asked to see Father Thomas and was told to wait. After what seemed an interminable time the monk who had befriended him appeared.

"What are you doing here at this hour, Joseph? It's very late," Father Thomas asked in surprise.

"May I come in, Father? It's important," Joseph pleaded.

"Come!" And the priest turned around and led the way to his cell. He motioned Joseph to the chair, but Joseph remained standing, while the Father sat on the edge of the cot. "What is it?" he asked quietly.

Joseph spoke rapidly: "I believe it is my destiny to serve God. I tried to fulfill this destiny through the rabbinate, but I know now that this was not the way God wanted me to serve. He had a different route for me to follow."

"Now just a minute, Joseph." This kind of talk was disturbing. "You are very agitated. I want you to go home and get a good night's sleep."

"No! Don't you see? God wants me to become a priest."

"A priest!"

"Yes! I shall become a Capuchin monk. I know now that this is why I was sent to Rome, this is why I met you and the novices, why I met the pope."

"My dear Joseph," the monk interrupted, "you are very upset, and your words are irrational. Don't you realize what this means?"

"It doesn't matter."

"You will become an apostate in the eyes of the Jewish community. You will be considered a pariah."

"I believe I already am."

"I know that you love your family, but this will cause them much suffering. Go home and make peace with your family before it is too late."

"No! I cannot!"

"You are very disturbed tonight, my son. Go home!"

"Father, this *is* my home. Today I had a revelation." And he proceeded to recount to the astonished priest the incident of the illusion in the park.

CHAPTER XXV

Joseph was led to a small cell, a room six feet in height, and with barely enough room to hold a cot, a narrow dresser and a small wooden table and chair. It also contained a sink, but no other plumbing. He would have to share the toilet, which was located at the end of the corridor, with the monks who were also housed on that floor. There was no light in the room, except for a dim flickering light that emanated from a candle and wick, which rested on the table. The cot was neatly made up, and someone brought him an extra blanket. He took off his shoes, but otherwise remained fully dressed. And then he lay down on the cot and covered himself up with the blanket. It was only when his head sank into the pillow that he began to realize the magnitude of what he had done.

"My family will hate me, my father will renounce me, my mother will weep, my brother and sister will never speak to me again, and my uncle will curse me." Such were his first thoughts. He prepared a mental balance sheet of his life. "What have I lost? Everything! I can never return to my home. I am consigned to the wilderness, banished. I have no money no support, no resources. What about the future? I can never acquire any wealth, for I shall have to take a vow of poverty. I will never have a wife, and I shall never know the joy of having children."

"What have I gained? For one thing, friends! For another, the respect of my peers! Most important; self-knowledge. I will discover my soul. And I will come closer to God." "Yet I know that I will rue this day. But something inside me tells me that I am doing the right thing, the only thing. I know that I was meant to be an ecclesiast, if not a rabbi, then a priest.

The old man tore the lapel of his jacket, rubbed his hands in charcoal and then blackened his face and covered his hair with soot. "My son is dead," he bewailed. "We shall sit Shiva and mourn his passing." He then began to recite the Hebrew prayer for the, dead: *'Yisgadal v'Yiskadash shmai rabo'*. Mama clung to him and begged,

"Don't, Rudy, I beg you, don't."

The tormented father cried: "Joseph, our youngest, is dead. His name is never to be brought up in this household again. His memory is to be blotted out." Thus did Papa greet the news that Joseph had converted to Christianity and become a Capuchin monk.

CHAPTER XXVI

The knock at the door was propitious. "Come in," said Calman, "the door is unlocked." The door was pushed open and the three ladies filed in, each carrying a tray laden with goodies.

Ruth immediately sensed the somber mood in the room and tried to introduce some levity. She started singing from the Gilbert and Sullivan operata, The Mikado - "Three little maids from school are we." The women then placed on the desk six pairs of colorful cups and saucers from Ruth's collection of odd chinaware together with a tray containing biscuits, croissants, cookies and jams, and a teapot. Ruth said:

"You gentlemen are too serious. It is time for a break." Malka was pouring a cup of tea for Calman, when a little head peered from behind the door.

"Mommy, I have to go to the bathroom," came Elizabeth's plaintive voice. "I will take her," said Helena, taking a couple of cookies and reaching for the child's hand. The somber mood that had prevailed before the arrival of the women had now changed into one of lightheartedness. Helena, who had no children of her own, was happy to have gained the little girl's confidence.

"How old are you?" she asked the child as she transported the cookies to her hand.

"Four and a half."

"Four and a half?" Helena repeated in mock surprise, "Almost five…my, you are getting to be a big girl." She then led the little one to her bedroom, tucked her in, gave her a kiss and a hug, and left. She heard Elizabeth call after her,

"Auntie Helen, I love you." Helena returned to the adult company beaming. The women poured tea for themselves, and occupied a couch in the room. Malka said, "We want to hear the rest of your conversation, and we're not leaving.

Fass took up where Stern had left off: "We learned that Joseph had become a Capuchin monk, and was known as Father John. One day, a few years after Joseph had left home, Malka needed to do some shopping and I decided to accompany her downtown. As we were crossing the street I espied two monks dressed in coarse brown robes walking on the side, which we were approaching.

I gasped, "Look, isn't that Joseph?" Malka also saw him and started to quaver. Almost at the same time he saw us. He waved to us and started walking briskly towards us, smiling. I grabbed Malka by the elbow, and we turned around and walked rapidly away from him, as if he were a leper. Later we were ashamed of our actions. We told Mama about the incident of the near encounter with Joseph, and she said, "Don't tell Papa. He will be very upset." But we discovered later, that for months afterwards Mama would go downtown every day hoping for a glimpse of her lost son.

The year 1938 saw the beginning of overt measures to destroy the Jews of Germany. The enactment of the Nuremberg Laws was a signal to the Nazis to impose ever-increasing restrictions on Jewish economic and cultural activity, including the closing down of the Jewish press, and many other harsh measures, culminating with the Kristallnacht in November of that year. The windows of Jewish shops were smashed and their goods looted. Those who tried to resist were either killed or beaten. Many were arrested and charged with instigating a riot. And the fines on the Jews were heavy.

Miklos Horty, who ruled Hungary as if he were an absolute monarch, was nothing more than a puppet of Hitler, and he had no choice but to bend to the will of his master. However, the rampant anti-Semitism of Germany and Austria had not yet become full-scale in Hungary, and Papa did not believe it ever would. His attitude was 'don't make waves' 'just ignore it and it will go away'. However, the problem was becoming graver by the day. Business began to decline, until it was but a trickle of what it had been. Finally, we began to realize together with the remainder of the Hungarian Jewish community, that danger was present, and we made it a policy not to go out, nor to open the doors after sunset.

One evening in February 1939 the family was gathered together at Papa and Mama's home. It was their forty-fifth wedding anniversary. We tried to instill some cheer into the celebration, but an aura of despair prevailed and the toasts, instead of to the long life of Mama and Papa, were to the liquidation of Hitler and the ending of the Jewish nightmare. Dinner was now finished and the table was being cleared, when the bell rang.

"Shh!" Papa whispered, "turn down the lamps."

"I wonder who could be calling so late," Mama said fearfully.

"Shh! Keep your voice to a whisper. Turn off the lights." The bell rang a second time. Everyone was silent. Then there was a pounding at the door. Again Papa whispered, "Do not answer the door." Then from the other side of the door a voice proclaimed the Hebrew exhortation: "*Sh'ma Ysroel (Hear O'Israel) Adoinoi alohanu Adoinoi echod* (the Lord our God, the Lord is One)."

Papa said in a low voice: "Emerich, answer the door, and may God have mercy on us." Emerich went forward and opened the door. In the framework of the door loomed the silhouette of a robed and hooded figure. The figure moved forward into the house, the door was shut and locked, and the lamps were turned on again. The figure removed his hood, and Joseph stood in the home he had left ten years ago. We stared at him transfixed. Mama let out a cry and stretched out her hands towards him, but Papa pulled her back.

The priest spoke: "In Germany and Austria, Jews are being sent to concentration camps, where they are forced into hard labor. They are being systematically starved and exposed to diseases. They are also being used for medical experiments. When their usefulness for these purposes is ended they are gassed and their bodies cremated. These poor people could have gotten out of the country two years ago, and gone to a safe haven. But they did not believe that this could happen in a civilized country, and they wanted to hold onto their valuables and their way of life. Now it is too late for them. They have lost everything, including their lives. I have come to tell you that Hungary is next. Rabbi Herskovits, Rabbi Schulz, Rabbi Shtern and all the rabbis of Hungary together have no power here, the church is powerless to help, and even Horty cannot save the Hungarian Jews. The power in this country belongs to the *'megbolondultol'*, the madmen. Hitler is under constant pressure from Eichman to set up concentration camps in Hungary, and this step in Hitler's solution is a certainty...just a matter of time. But it is not too late for you to escape. I can help you now. In one year's time it will be too late. Start to sell off your possessions, and I can arrange for you to settle in Australia, America or even South Africa, where you will be safe. It will be too dangerous for me to make direct contact with you again, so the next time you hear from me it will be through an intermediary. You will know of me by the name of Father John. Goodbye." He turned and left.

Emerich shut the door behind him. We all remained standing in silence for some time. Then Papa found his voice: "I do not make deals with ghosts."

"But Papa," said Malka, "it was Joseph, and he wants to help."

"No," he replied. "We did not see Joseph. Joseph is dead. Whatever we experienced, it was an illusion."

In 1942 Goebbels, the infamous propagandist had brain-washed nearly all of Germany with his baneful propaganda, and his accomplice, Eichman, had persuaded Hitler that the time was overdue to spew their vilification of the Jews into Hungary, as part of the 'final solution'. Miklos Kallasz, the Hungarian Prime Minister, and flunky for his German superiors, was only too happy to oblige. He ordered the expropriation of Jewish property. Still, the Shtern and Fass families made no move to leave their homes.

Little by little we fell into a lethargic state of acceptance of our intolerable situation. Every day we heard new tales of the murder of Hungarian Jews by the SS and Hungarian troops. But we remained as in a trance, and did nothing to save ourselves. This is the closest we had ever come to Hell.

1944. In Germany the smell of defeat was in the air. The inner circle of the Reichstag was becoming concerned about rumors of an assassination attempt. And the heinous Goebbels was worried that he would not be able to fulfill his obsession to wipe out all the Jews. His right-hand aide, Eichman, was not satisfied with the rate of deportation of Jews from Hungary to the German concentration camps. So he ordered the deportation of four hundred thousand Jews to Auschwitz, and sent German troops into Hungary to ensure his orders were being carried out. However the Catholic Church was still a power to be reckoned with in Hungary.

Joseph, Father John, using the authority of his robe and hood, returned once more to his old home. Papa had grown thin and his face was sallow. Mama was old and frail. The remainder of the family looked worn, our clothes frayed, we all needed dental work. When Joseph entered the house, no one acted surprised. Even papa was resigned. But he made one last effort to assert his authority:

"What do you want with us, heathen?"

Joseph looked him straight in the eyes, and confronting the old man said:

"Listen to me, all of you. You have rejected my offers of help, and turned away my messengers." He held father's gaze as if by a beam. Papa could not turn away. "Uncle Avrum, your brother, Rabbi Stern and his wife, Tante Hanna have been seized by the Nazis, and are being sent to the camps." Papa let out a low sob. "His son, your nephew, Herzl, has taken refuge in my monastery and shares my cell. Now hear this. You are all on the list…all of you. You are marked for death. The SS will be here imminently…today perhaps, not later than tomorrow. The monastery cannot take any more refugees. But I have arranged for a nunnery to take you in. You must come now. There is no time to lose." Now Papa took control again as in past years.

"Children," he said, "Emeric, Helena, Gula, Malka, go to your rooms and pack a few essentials, and go with your brother, Yojikam." When he uttered Joseph's Hebrew name, we all experienced a moment of dread, followed by relief.

"What about you and Mama?" asked Emerich.

"Go!" he ordered.

Papa turned back to Joseph: "Do you remember the story of Joseph, son of Jacob and Rachel, who was sold into slavery, only to rise up as one of Pharaoh's most trusted leaders, and who saved the very family who had rejected him? Today you have fulfilled this prophecy." Papa wept as he embraced his son at last. "God forgive me for what I have done."

Joseph said to him: "Papa, you did that which was allotted to you by God."

Papa still clinging to him asked: "Father, do you forgive me?"

And Joseph replied, "Father, I do."

"Malka and I were the first to come down. It was mildly warm outside, but I was wearing a gray tweed jacket and hat to match, heavy woolen stockings and hiking boots. In one hand I carried a satchel containing a shirt, a change of underwear, a sweater, some soap and shaving accessories. In the other hand I carried the Malacca cane, which had belonged to my late father, Pavel, of blessed memory. Malka, too, was dressed for colder weather, and she carried a twin satchel. Malka reproached her father: "Papa why are you dawdling? Quick! Go upstairs and pack your things. You too mama!"

Emerich appeared at the top of the stairs. He was dressed in his best suit - a black serge with double-breasted jacket, a white shirt, black silk tie and diamond pin, leather black well-shined shoes. Over one hand was draped a short black cloth coat. In the other hand he carried a duffel bag. Helena followed behind, dressed in a subdued flower-patterned skirt, also carrying a duffel bag. They descended the stairs, and like his sister, Emerich found fault with his parents:

"Mama...Papa, what are you waiting for? We have to go." Helena stood back, her fingertips pressed to her lips in reflective mode. She had never seen her father-in-law in such a serene state. Here was a man who, if he did not move quickly, might be dead by the end of this day. Yet he seemed at peace with himself and the world. She understood the premonition that now gripped her. She went over to him and kissed him on the cheek, tears welling in her eyes.

"Good-bye, Papa."

"Goodbye," he said sadly. Papa turned to Emerich. He was no longer the family patriarch, giving orders, but spoke kindly and resignedly, just above a whisper: "Emerichel," which was a term of endearment, and he removed his son's diamond pin and handed it back to him,

"Hide this in your bag, or it will be stolen." He then walked to the safe and opened it. He withdrew a number of precious gems and began to distribute them to the family members.

"When you get out of Hungary you will need these to buy your way. Keep them well hidden." He turned to me.

"Emerich is the oldest, and I pass on the responsibility to him. If anything happens to him I know you are very capable." He turned to Joseph, "Father John, the rest of these valuables belong to you."

"No. I cannot. I have taken a vow of poverty."

"Then take them for the church to whom we now owe so much. Better than they should fall into the hands of the Nazis."

Malka began to cry: "Papa, why aren't you and Mama coming with us?"

Mama clung to Papa's arm:

"I stay with Papa. Where he goes I go."

Papa said: "Now stop whimpering. LEAVE!"

We walked out of the house and turned back for a last glimpse of Papa and Mama.

"Emerich," Papa called, "just a minute." Emerich retraced his steps towards Papa, who handed him his ebony cane.

CHAPTER XXVII

Stern asked: "Is it all right if I smoke?" Calman passed him an ashtray and took the opportunity to fill his own pipe.

Someone asked: "Is the coffee still warm?"

Ruth said, "I'll make a fresh pot," and she took the pot into the kitchen. Malka accompanied her.

"You have a comfortable house here, Ruth," she commented, "how long have you lived here?"

"Let me see. We bought it one year after we were married. So we've lived here nearly seven years."

"Are you still working?" Malka enquired.

"No," she answered, "but I'm thinking of doing some private counseling. Cal has agreed to let me use his den as an office."

"Was it you I saw on the television talking about your work?"

"It probably was! A group of us were interviewed two weeks ago on marriage counseling methods."

"I watched the program because I thought I recognized you."

"You know, Malka," Ruth told her, "before Cal and I were married and for a year afterwards I worked extensively with Jewish Holocaust survivors who had immigrated to Canada. If I can help you in any way…"

Malka interrupted her and placed a hand on her arm. "Someday I would like to come see you."

"Tell me what happened to you when you were in the nunnery." "It is hard for me to speak about it but I will try.

"Joseph led us to the nunnery and introduced us to the Mother Superior. She was very kind, and apologized because the four of us would have to share one room. The room was large and clean, but the furniture was sparse, and consisted of four cots, a plain rough-grained wooden table and two benches. There was no bathroom. There was not even a wash-basin. If we wanted to use these facilities we had to go to the other end of the hallway. There was always a lineup waiting to get in.

"Then, after we had been in our hiding place in the nunnery for nearly three weeks, a novice nun came timidly into the room followed by two Jewish couples. "I'm sorry," she said, "but you'll have to share your room with these lovely people," and she introduced them—the Farkases and the Bogdars.

"As the weeks went by the Nazis intensified their search for Jews, and our physical condition worsened as more refugees were crowded into our quarters, until, finally, we were eighteen souls sharing the room. We only had the four cots, so we rotated, each of us getting to use a cot one day in four. During the rest of the time we slept on the floor. My poor brother, Emerich, suffered terrible pain from an old back injury he had received during the First World War. At the beginning we used to go outside in the courtyard to exercise every day. But now it was too dangerous to step beyond the confines of the nunnery. The SS were everywhere, and we remained confined to our room, which was permeated by a foul odor resulting from bodily functions, which we could not always control.

"In March, 1945 we heard a rumor that the Russians were getting closer and were planning an offensive drive, and that we could hope to be liberated soon. But we had also heard that the Russians committed atrocities as bad as the Germans, and our feelings of hope were mixed with ominous forebodings. And then we learned that two monks had been arrested by the Nazis and charged with aiding Jews. The older man, Father Thomas, had already been executed. The younger, Father John, was being held for questioning, which meant torture. Three weeks later the Russian army entered, and the Nazis scattered like rats. Father John, my brother Joseph, had been subjected to torture but had not given up our secret. When the Nazis fled they dared not kill a priest for fear of reprisals." The coffee pot had begun to gurgle, and the ladies returned to the study with fresh coffee.

CHAPTER XXVIII

Stern continued: "By April, 1945 the Russian army had liberated all of Hungary. There was singing and rejoicing in the streets. We had survived, and together the four of us—Gula, Malka, Helena and I—returned to our home in trepidation. We found the house to be in good shape, and we learned that three German officers and their mistresses had occupied it until two days before. They had broken the safe, but of course we had already cleaned it out. They ruined the piano and left the bedding in a mess, but there was little further damage. There was no pilferage, but, then, what could they have pilfered? We went into Mama and Papa's bedroom, and searched the rest of the house and grounds, but could find no clue of what might have happened to them. We scoured the neighborhood and called on every home in the vicinity. Eventually we learned that Mama and Papa, may their memories be a blessing, had been arrested by the Gestapo within hours after we had said our farewells. They were sent off to Auschwitz, where they perished.

"Hell is to be locked up—eighteen people in a single room with no toilets. Heaven is to have your own room and to be able to loll in a warm bath. As summer approached we sunbathed amongst the flowers in the back yard. We reopened the jewelry store but business was not good. No one had any money. The forint had replaced the pengo as currency, and that was in short supply. But what did that matter? We were alive, and life was good.

"Then came the most wonderful news—Malka was pregnant. Gula reopened his father's old business, bottling syrups and fruit beverages. Once each month, on a Friday evening, Joseph joined us for the Sabbath dinner. However, we no longer called him Joseph, but Father John. During these special evenings we had pleasant reminiscences, and it was at these dinners that we learned about Father Thomas and his sacrifice, and Joseph's meeting up with the seminarians on his way to Rome, and his revelation in the park.

"Those Hungarians who had committed atrocities against the Jews, especially their helping in the deportation to the death camps, were arrested and put on trial. But Jewish property that had been seized was never returned. Though now banned, there was still latent anti-Semitism, and we heard of pogroms occurring here and there. Hungary became a people's republic in 1949 after the communist party came into power, and things once more began to look bad for the Jews, We were worried that the few assets we did have would be confiscated, and this time when Joseph advised us to leave Hungary we listened to him. It was decided that we would make application to the Canadian embassy for permission to immigrate to Canada. As you know, Helena and I came here in 1950, and Gula and Malka waited to wind up their business, and they arrived here a year later."

CHAPTER XXIX

Calman looked at his watch. It was getting late. He focused his attention on Stern and Fass: "Gentlemen, I have a number of clients who immigrated to Canada after the war from diverse parts of Europe – Czechoslovakia, Yugoslavia, Latvia, Poland, Austria, Holland, Denmark, even Germany, and, of course, Hungary. Each one of them has a moving story. Yours, I think, is the most poignant. But when you came here this evening I thought…I hoped you had come to explain the millions of dollars that appeared in your bank account during the past three years. What you told me might make a sensitive tax auditor weep, but then he would have to charge you with tax evasion. I am frankly disappointed that your story ends here without further explanation."

"Did we say that this is the end?" Fass interjected.

Cal again looked at his watch impatiently and said resignedly,

"All right! Let's have it."

Stern took over again: "Hungary fell under communist domination, and became a part of the Soviet bloc. Industry was nationalized and farm-land was collectivized. Religion in all forms was suppressed. Cardinal Mindszenty was arrested and put on trial, despite the protests around the world. Jewish institutions were closed and many activists were arrested.

There was an economic crisis. Thank God we were already safe in Canada. In 1956 came the Hungarian Revolution. The people struck back against the oppressive Soviet regime. Hungarians escaped by the thousands, many of whom found their way to Canada, and many of these settled right here in Toronto. But armed guards heavily patrolled the Hungarian borders. Those who got out were lucky to escape with their lives, far less, their possessions. But, through the underground, word got out that there was a priest who could help them to salvage some of their valuables."

In December 1956 we received a surprise visit from our brother, Father John. Yes, he came all the way from Hungary to see us. He was introduced to the children, who were in awe of him. And we had a great feast and celebration. He slept over at our apartment on the first night, but for the remainder of his stay he quartered at a nearby monastery. On that first evening I asked him how he had managed to get out of Hungary and how he proposed to get back in.

"That was not too difficult," he told us, "as a priest I have special traveling privileges. The church is powerful, and the communists want to avoid confrontations, especially after the Mindszenty affair." Father John spent a few days with us getting acclimatized to our new home, our new country and our new life style. Then he told us the real purpose of his visit.

"I am afraid I will have to cut short my stay with you," he said.

"Why," we asked him, "Why not stay here in Canada? It is a beautiful country, and there is so much to see, and here there is freedom."

"You see," he replied, "I am actually here on a special mission."

"Oh," I asked him, "is this mission a secret or can we be let in on it?"

"Both," he replied. "Many Hungarians, especially those with wealth, are on a death list because they have resisted the communists, and they are trying to escape to another country. But the borders are well guarded and they are lucky to get out with the clothes on their back. Even if they could hide money on their persons, Hungarian currency has no value outside the country. Quite a number of these people have come to me for help. They bring me their valuables—paintings, icons, stamp and coin collections, manuscripts—which I am able to transport out of the country in my courier's pouch."

"What would happen to you if you were caught?" I asked him. He smiled,

"It would mean, as they say in America 'curtains'…Kaput."

"And what happens with these objects?" I enquired.

"I take them to Tangiers, where I have a contact, a reliable art dealer, who gives me a fair valuation for each piece. I then travel to Berne or Geneva where I put them out to auction with a guaranteed minimum price, based on the values given to me by my friend from Tangiers."

He continued: "The funds are then sent from Geneva to a secret contact in Paris, from where they are routed to London. In London they are deposited in Barclays bank, where, after a few weeks we draw a draft in U. S. funds, and these funds are relayed to a contact in New York.

"Yes, we follow you?" I said, fidgeting about in my chair. "And then what happens?"

"The funds are held for distribution in an American bank. Have you heard of the Chase Manhattan Bank?" Calman listened in astonishment, as he began to see the light.

"I'm wondering why you don't just allocate the sale proceeds to the final recipients directly from Berne," I said.

"Because," he replied, "the KBG are everywhere, and they are clever and ruthless, the same as the SS used to be. If they discovered what I was up to they would block every loophole in the scheme, and they would likely kill me, and the lives of my church brothers would be in jeopardy. The purpose of this moving about from place to place is to confuse them, to sort of set up a smoke screen, which we hope they will not be able to penetrate. Do you follow me?"

"Yes! You want to keep them off the scent."

"Precisely!"

"Yes! I've heard of the Chase Manhattan." We needed some time to absorb all that we had heard.

After some time I broke the silence:

"Do you remember the Chum book that Papa gave us when we were young?" I asked him.

"You mean the one that his uncle had given him when he was a boy? The one with all the adventure stories?"

"Yes! That's the one!"

"We always wanted to live out those stories."

"We did live them out in our imagination."

"And now," Gula chimed in, "here you are, living them out in the real world." Joseph smiled in recollection and I added: "A regular Robin Hood."

"Well," Father John continued, "as you are aware Canada has become a principal haven for our people, and many Hungarians have settled here, mainly in Vancouver, Montreal and Toronto."

Emeric thought for a while, and then shifting closer to his brother, said conspiratorially, "And so you want us to be the Canadian contact?"

"Yes! That is my reason for coming here to Canada. Many Hungarians have found refuge here in this great land of yours, and many more will be emigrating from Hungary to Canada."

"What would be involved?" I asked.

"You would be receiving funds from New York, and would be processing them to the proper claimants. But, before you give me an answer I want you to think about it carefully. It could be dangerous." Emeric said reflectively,

"I would like to discuss your proposal with Gula and Malka and my wife. Is that all right?"

"Yes, but time is pressing and I must return to Hungary before I arouse suspicion with my absence. Do you think you could let me know by tomorrow?"

The next day the two of us—Gula and I—sat down in my apartment with my brother, Father John, to talk about the plan. Gula asked him: "When we receive the money how will we know to whom we should disburse it, and how much we should disburse to each person?"

"That part is easy. You should open a separate bank account for this purpose. You will notify the New York contact of the bank account number, and he will from time to time wire funds into this account. A few days before the funds are sent you will receive a list consisting of code numbers and amounts. Only you and I will know the identity of the code number. When you contact those persons they will identify themselves by yet another code number, and then you will give them the proceeds due to them according to the New York list. Once you have paid these people it would best if you had no further contact with them."

Calman stretched his arms above his head. "Wow! So that explains it all—where the money came from and where it all went. Were you paid a fee for this?"

"No! Even if we were offered to be paid for our work we would not accept."

"You know," Calman declared, "I could not believe you were involved in any dishonest scheme, but I couldn't imagine anything like this.

An emotional Gula Fass now declared: "We will not tell this to that taxman, Petroman…"

"Peterson," Cal corrected him. "Yes, that man. We will not jeopardize the life of the man who saved our lives. Better I should go to jail."

The three men remained behind while the women cleared the dishes and straightened out the room. Emeric and Julius lit up cigarettes and Calman filled his pipe with an aromatic tobacco, tamped it down, and also lit up.

"There must be a way to get off the horns of this dilemma," Calman mused. He stroked his chin.

"Let me sleep on it. In fact, it's pretty late now. Go home, and we'll talk tomorrow, and, by the way, thanks for confiding in me, and Mr. Stern, don't forget your cane."

CHAPTER XXX

Calman did not sleep well that night. He tossed and turned, and finally, at 4 a.m. he got up, went into the kitchen and brewed a cup of tea.

Ruth heard him fussing there, and she too got up, put on her dressing gown, and joined him. "Would you like some toast with the jam that the Sterns brought us?" she asked him. He nodded. They nibbled at the toast and drank the tea silently, and then Ruth asked, "So, what do you think?"

"I don't really know what to think," he replied.

"Well, now, suppose you were to explain what happened to the tax auditor. Wouldn't he be sympathetic?"

"I don't think so," Calman replied, "he's young and, from my short conversations with him, I think he's immature, anxious for a kill. I guess he thinks that would mean a promotion."

"Oh dear me," Ruth exclaimed, "could you speak to our member of parliament?"

"No, he's a back-bencher who never says a word, an innocuous toady who votes at the party's call. This case is loaded. He wouldn't know how to unload it."

"Cal, didn't you vote for him?"

"Not I. Did you?"

"I don't remember."

"However, Ruth, you've given me an idea. What if I were to call the Minister of Finance? I would request an interview. I would tell him the story in strict confidence, and wouldn't disclose any names. What do you think of that?"

"Well, he may refuse to give you an interview. After all, he's a very busy man. You may still have to get to see him through our M.P., so don't write him off yet."

Calman Mencher arrived at his office at 9:30 a.m. He greeted the staff with a smile and a yawn. Someone said, "Oh! Oh! Here come de boss, and he's late."

Alec quipped: "Good afternoon, Cal. Did you sleep well this morning?" Cal ignored him. But there was an easy atmosphere in the office, and everybody was called by their given names, except in the presence of a client, when it was 'Mr. Mencher'. Cal sat down at his desk, and Audrey followed with a cup of steaming coffee.

"I left a folder of checks for you to sign. How about getting them out of the way before you start?" Calman took out his pen and opened the folder. "Did you remember that you have an appointment with Mr. Marton at eleven o'clock this morning? I've put his file on your desk."

"Yes, I remember," he said, as he commenced going through the folder. "Audrey, I want you to try to get me the Minister of Finance."

"In Ottawa?" she asked surprised.

"Yes, in Ottawa!"

"Who is the minister?"

"I'm not sure. It may be Fleming." Fifteen minutes later Calman's buzzer sounded, "Yes Audrey."

"Cal, it's impossible to get through to the Minister, but I got someone in the office of the ministry. Do you want to talk to her? "Yes! O.K. Put her on."

"Allo," came a feminine francophone voice, "can I 'elp you?"

"Yes, thank you for taking my call. My name is Calman Mencher. I'm a chartered accountant, practicing in Toronto. I have here a most unusual tax situation. The reason I would like to have an appointment with the Minister is that I believe this case has national, indeed, international implications."

"Just a minute!" Several minutes elapsed before a polite male voice came on the phone.

"Good morning, sir. What seems to be the problem?" Calman repeated his request. The gentleman on the other line seemed to know his business.

"I'm sorry, sir," he said, "but if this is a matter of national importance you should be talking to the Justice Department. If it is a matter pertaining to a taxpayer, you will want to talk to the Ministry of National Revenue… not the Ministry of Finance. "

"Thank you," said Calman, "Can you give me the name of the Minister of National Revenue?"

"That would be the Honorable Paul Hellyer."

"I'll try, but you might get cut off." Calman was cut off.

"Damn," Calman murmured to himself, "I should have known I had the wrong department."

The intercom buzzed and Audrey picked up the phone: "Yes, Cal?" There was a pause. She continued: "Were you able to get an appointment?"

"No, I had the wrong department. Try to get me Paul Hellyer. It's the Minister of National Revenue we want, not the Minister of Finance."

"O.K!" Ten minutes later Calman's phone buzzed again.

"You're on," Audrey said.

"Mr. Minister?" Calman intoned.

"No, no, this is an aide to the minister...Mr. Campion. How can I help you?"

"First, thank you for taking my call..." Then Calman recounted to him the nature of the call as he had to the Finance Ministry. Campion listened patiently, and then replied,

"Unfortunately, the minister will be away for a conference, starting tomorrow, and on his return he has a full slate of appointments. Let me see if there is some way to fit you in. I assume you will come to Ottawa?"

"Oh, yes, yes...at the minister's convenience."

"All right, I will call you back. Let me have your phone number." Calman hung up the phone smiling, as the door to his office swung open. Audrey slid in and closed the door behind her.

"You look like Calamity Jane," he joked.

"He's here," she said concernedly.

"Who's here?" "The *Malachovitz*"

"Who?"

"The Angel of Death!"

"The Angel of Death?" he laughed.

"Worse," she hissed, "it's Peterson." Calman was still smiling,

"O. K. Show him in."

A young man entered the office. Calman estimated his age at twenty-one. He was tall and awkward in his gait, he had a sallow complexion, his hairline was receding, and one could detect white specks of dandruff on the shoulders and neckline of his jacket. Calman extended his hand in greeting, and they shook hands. His hands were damp.

"A fish," Calman mused. "Would you care for a coffee?" Calman offered.

"No, I don't drink coffee." Peterson speculated to himself, *This guy is already trying to bribe me with coffee.* Calman was baiting him, "Perhaps you would care for a whisky?"

"I don't drink." The irony had escaped the young man.

"Would you care for a glass of water?"

"No!"

"What, not even water?" This time Peterson was smart enough not to reply.

Calman continued officiously, "Mr. Peterson, please correct me if I'm wrong, but my calendar does not show that we have an appointment to-day."

"We don't have an appointment, but you did not return my phone calls." He was getting sharp.

Calman said calmly,

"That is true, but I had already told you I would get back to you in May."

"Well, it's May 3rd. Do you want me to leave?" He was being antagonistic.

"No," Calman kept his temper, "I think we can deal with your request here. But before I show you the bank pass book which you're so anxious to examine I want to know why you want to see it?"

Peterson replied, still angry: "As a tax auditor I have the right to investigate any financial transactions of a taxpayer."

"I suppose that, as a general rule that is true, more or less. But I am curious to know how you found out about the existence of the account?"

"We have our way of finding cheaters, and I will not disclose our source."

"Are you implying that my client is a cheater?" Now Calman was beginning to show anger. But Peterson held his ground.

"You have been doing your best to frustrate my investigation, and yes, I think we have caught a tax fraud right here in your office."

A very angry Mencher stood up and pointed his finger at Peterson: "And you have been harassing my office as well as my client. I want the name and phone number of your supervisor." The buzzer sounded.

"It's the Ministry of National Revenue," Audrey piped in. Calman made sure that the speaker was on so that Peterson could hear the conversation. "Thank you. Hello Mr. Minister?"

"No. It's Mr. Campion. I'm sorry, Mr. Mencher, but the Minister will simply be unable to see you. However, I have made an appointment for you with the Deputy Minister this Thursday. Could you be here at 9:30 a.m."

"Yes, can you give me the address?"

"Do you know where the Lisgar Building is?"

"Yes, it so happens I do."

"Come to the second floor. And good luck." Calman returned the phone to its cradle and turned back to Peterson. "The name of your supervisor," he repeated.

"Why do you want that?" A nervous Peterson knew he had gone too far, and was now on the defensive.

"Because you are too immature to be in charge of this file, and I don't want to deal with the likes of you. You have come here with a biased attitude. You have not even looked at the facts, but you have already decided that my client is guilty of some infraction. You know what! Don't trouble yourself. I'll find out the name of your supervisor and pay him a call. When you leave, my office will you be good enough to close the door behind you."

Peterson started to say something, but Calman had already opened a new file, and had buzzed Audrey. He looked up impatiently and threateningly and the tax auditor returned a pasty and scared look. He turned around and walked out of Calman's office.

CHAPTER XXXI

Ruth had laid out Calman's white shirt, the one with the French cuffs, and his favorite cufflinks, the gold ones with his initials engraved on them which she had bought for him on his last birthday. She had also ironed the trousers of his blue serge suit and hung up the suit where he would have quick access to it. She placed his blue tie displaying the University of Toronto logo, on the dresser.

Calman was up at five-thirty a.m. He dressed quickly as Ruth got up and made him a cup of tea with toast. He dunked the toast and gulped down the coffee, seized his briefcase and dashed out the door. In a moment he was back.

"What did you forget?" Ruth asked him. He took her in his arms and kissed her warmly on the lips. She kissed him back.

"Now, I'm all set," he said, and got into his car.

The plane landed at 8:05 a.m. at the Ottawa International Airport. Calman entered one of the waiting cabs. "Lisgar Building," he said crisply.

"Did you say Lisgar Building?" The cabbie asked.

"Yes! The Lisgar Building."

"Are you sure that's where you wanna go? You sure you want the Lisgar?

"Why? Don't you know how to get there?"

"What're ya gonna do at the ol' Lisgar Building?"

Calman ignored him. *Busy-body*, he thought to himself.

"Don't you know they're demolishing the building?"

"Maybe, but not before I've had my meeting."

"O.K. But I think they've already started to tear it down. You won't be able to get in." Calman was a little alarmed at this information. He looked at the address and telephone directory he carried in his briefcase to make certain he had the phone number of Mr. Campion.

"Hey! Who did you say you're meeting with?"

"I didn't say! And it's none of your business." After a pause, "I'm meeting with one of the ministries."

"Huh! They're ain't no government officials at the Lisgar anymore. You got the wrong place. They've all moved out. You'll see."

"Where are they moving to?"

"I think Banks Street."

"Well, take me to the Lisgar anyhow." Calman paid the driver as they arrived in front of the Lisgar.

"Do you want me to wait just in case?"

"No, thank you! That won't be necessary."

Calman emerged from the cab in front of the Lisgar and stepped back to survey the old building. He remembered it from his Air Force days in 1943 and 1944, when it was headquarters for the R.C.A.F. He had twenty minutes to spare, and walked into the first floor of the building, but was unable to identify his old office. All the partitions had been removed, and even the demising walls had been demolished. There were no desks, no files, and no furniture of any kind. The place had been swept clean.

Calman began to worry: *My God, the cab driver was right. The damn place is empty.* He took the stairs two at a time to the second landing. Except for a few cartons, which were being loaded onto carts the place seemed vacant, a monstrous cavern. Calman estimated that the area had to be forty thousand square feet. The windows were grimy. They had not been cleaned in months, maybe years. This was the floor on which his meeting was to take place. He began to wonder: *Is this some kind of joke?* He started walking down the floor. About two-thirds of the way down he passed a squat man seated on an old swivel chair, behind an even older, dilapidated desk, with both feet resting on the desk, one crossed over the other. He noted that one shoe displayed a hole in the sole, through which the man's sock could be seen. *A Dickensonian character*, Calman mused. Above the desk hung a light bulb, which was suspended from the ceiling by a cord. The bulb was protected be a green shade. On the desk he observed two tumblers and a bottle of Seagram's Rye.

Calman continued to walk down the large room looking for some sign of activity. He saw two workmen loading cartons onto a handcart and approached them: "Excuse me," he asked: "are there any offices remaining on this floor?"

"No," replied one of the men, "this big space is the whole floor."

"What's going on here?"

"Oh! They're demolishing the building. Our company has the contract. I don't think you should be here."

As a last chance, pointing to the man seated at the desk, whom he had passed, Calman asked them: "Can you tell me who that man is?"

Again the same fellow replied, "I don't know. He's been there for half an hour. Maybe he's here to check things out. But we're going to have to ask him to move soon."

Calman retraced his steps to the seated man. As he came closer the man smiled at him and in a distinctive French Canadian accent asked him: "You are Monsieur Manché?"

"Menchér," Calman corrected his pronunciation. "Are you the deputy minister?"

"No," he said, "not exactly, but I am representing him today." Calman was now worried. What had he got himself into?

But he didn't want to get out of line with this man, so affecting nonchalance, he remarked in a quasi-question,

"I guess the deputy minister couldn't make it today?" The representative did not answer, but instead refilled his glass with whisky, and then filled the other glass, which he pushed over to Calman. He gestured him to pick up the proffered glass.

"Before we 'ave our talk, I tink I should introduce myself. My name is Lemieux, and I am dah parliamentary secretary." The relief showed on Calman's face, but the secretary took no notice. Calman tried to please him by speaking in French:

"Quel pleasir de vous connais." Lemieux smiled. "Shit," Calman screamed inwardly at himself, "high-school French."

"Monsieur Mancher…" Calman did not try to correct him again…please 'ave a drink, and den we will talk, but I t'ink we should speak in h'English. It will be better for de bote of us." Lemieux downed half of his glass while Calman politely took a couple of small sips. He tried to make small talk to put them both at ease. But he was also curious about this vulgar-looking man who laid claim to such high office.

"You hold a very high office, Sir," he said.

"Maybe so, but de pay is not so great."

"Well," Calman quipped, "those are the wages of politics." The words slipped out, and he prayed Lemieux would not make the association with the phrase 'wages of sin'.

But Lemieux was no fool, and he responded, "I t'ink der is a joke somewhere here. I t'ink also we should get down to our business before dey pack us into one of dose crates." He finished the contents of his glass and refilled. "Drink up," he said, clinking Calman's glass. Calman took another sip. "So, Monsieur Mancher, tell me de purpose of your visit."

Calman commenced: "Mr. Secretary, as you are aware, during the past several years a large number of Hungarian émigrés have entered Canada." The secretary nodded.

"Yes, I am aware!"

"They are, by and large, a cultured, proud and industrious people, and they are law-abiding. You will find that very few of them are on the unemployment rolls or that they are otherwise a burden to the government."

"Dat is true."

"Most of these people had to escape from a harsh communist regime, and many of them came away with barely the clothes on their backs. However, they needed funds to get started in their new country if they were not to be a burden. So, before making their escape from Hungary, they brought their portable valuables to a daring and benevolent priest, who, through an ingenious plan was able to channel these goods to foreign countries where they were auctioned and the proceeds returned to the rightful owners. The funds were routed through a number of countries and were transformed into a number of different currencies until they reached their final destination. A trusted individual was selected for each destination to hold the funds in trust until the rightful recipient was identified through an elaborate code. My client is that trustee for Canada."

"I see," said Monsieur Lemieux, refilling his near empty glass. He clinked Calman's glass again encouraging him to join him. This time Calman took a longer drink.

"Well, I see de problem. Some idiot from de tax department hav' discovered de trust account and 'e figure e' 'as come across a cache of undeclared income. Is dat right?"

Calman was astonished at the man's quick insight. "Sir, you have hit the nail on the head."

"Well, it is very simple. Why don't you tell him de troot?"

"That is precisely why I am here, Sir. My client is concerned to let out the secret, even to the most discreet individual. Even with a man of goodwill, which this auditor does not have towards my client, the secret might inadvertently become known. Then the game would be over, and this gentleman, this priest who has risked his life would be arrested and probably executed. I myself have pledged not to reveal the identity of my client."

The parliamentary secretary stood up now, clasped his hands behind his back, and paced back and forth, thinking. Calman was surprised that the man could stand up and walk in a straight line after all that drinking. He returned to the desk. There was half a glass of whisky left in the bottle. He poured it into his glass and gulped it down. He then turned to Calman, took him by the arm, and said: "If we do not leave, I am afraid dey will pack us into de cartons." He led Calman towards the door. "All right," he said, "go back to your client, and tell heem not to worry. He will not 'ear from this assessor again. De file is now closed."

Calman gasped: "But sir, you don't even know the name of the assessor, nor for that matter the identity of my client."

"Monsieur Mancher, I 'ave not asked you to tell me your secrets. Don't ask me to tell you mine."

Calman downed the balance of his drink in one gulp and shook hands. They left the building together.

EPILOGUE I

1981—Cal Mencher had just turned sixty, but he could find no reason to celebrate. Two years earlier his idol, Ruth, had passed on. Their friends at first invited him out to their homes but eventually grew tired of his grieving and stopped calling him. He spent much of his time revisiting the old haunts he and Ruth used to frequent, but it only increased his despair. He went regularly to her grave and placed yellow roses on the tombstone, but it did not alleviate his pain. He was not looking after himself, and his children were becoming alarmed. They wanted him to join them for his birthday celebration, but he had turned them down. He had taken to walking, sometimes for hours, and could be seen most evenings wearing a tweed hat, and if it were cool, a leather jacket and, sometimes, gloves, and carrying a cane.

Calman had left his home on a walking spree on a Saturday afternoon. It was almost 8 o'clock when he realized it had begun to drizzle, so he turned into a restaurant known for its fine dining. The maitre d' smiled at him.

"Table for one," he said.

"This way sir," and he led the way to a single table. Calman found himself seated in a comfortable chair, and took note with some pleasure of the crisp damask tablecloth and the elegant setting. The waiter approached him:

"Will you be having a drink this evening sir?" he asked pleasantly.

Calman reflected for a moment. "I think I would like a brandy. Do you have a Hennessey?"

"Why yes sir." The waiter seemed surprised. "Will you be having some wine as well?"

"No, thank you." Calman recalled his first date with Ruth at the Maison d'Or when he had ordered a Hennessey cognac. "Will you bring my brandy in a snifter please?"

"Yes sir!"

"By the way," Calman asked him, "where are your telephones?" The waiter pointed to the front of the restaurant, and Calman went off to phone his daughter, Elizabeth, to assure her that he was all right, and was dining out.

When he returned to his seat he noticed that a younger couple had been seated at a table across from him. They whispered something to one another, and then they both looked at him. They caught his eye and smiled and nodded. He smiled back and also nodded. He thought they looked familiar, but could not place them, and when the waiter brought his drink he dismissed them from his mind. He was reading the menu when the gentleman across stood up, walked over to his table, and addressed him:

"Excuse me, sir," he said, but aren't you Mr. Mencher?"

"Yes, I am," Calman replied, "and you look familiar, but I cannot recall where we met."

"I was Mr. Fass's son-in-law and this is my wife," indicating the lady, "who was his daughter." Her smile was broad and welcoming, and he thought she was very pretty, reminding him of her aunt, Helen Stern, whom he had not seen for some fifteen years. "Mr. Mencher, you seem to be alone this evening. Won't you join our table?"

Calman stood up, shook hands with the young man, and moved over to the next table, taking his cognac with him. Looking at the young woman, Calman said inquiringly,

"I do not understand what you mean when you say that you were Julius Fass's daughter. Why do you speak of him in the past tense?"

"Papa passed away about eight years ago," she replied sadly. Calman, visibly shaken and saddened, fumbled awkwardly, "I uh, I didn't know. I uh, I guess I lost touch with the family after they sold the business."

"Let me see," he mused, "that was about fourteen years ago. Your father must have already been ill at that time."

The waiter came by and took their orders.

"And your mother, how is she?"

"Oh, mama! She's fine. In fact, she lives with us."

"Please give her my regards and my belated condolences."

Calman let his hands warm the snifter, and then brought it up to his nostrils and ingested the aroma, before drinking. "And the Sterns," he added, "How are they?"

"Uncle Emeric passed away three months ago, but Aunt Helen is fine, except that she's a little forgetful."

"I'm very sorry about your uncle. He was a gentleman. And does your aunt live with you too?"

The man replied: "We've tried to get her to join us, but she's very independent. She still lives in the same apartment that they occupied when they first came to Canada."

"Let me see," said Calman, "that was about thirty years ago. You know, I think I would like to talk to her, perhaps pay her a visit. Do you have her phone number?"

EPILOGUE II

Cal pushed the bell button, and the door immediately flung open. There she stood— 'the face that launched the thousand ships'.

"Mr. Calman Mencher!" She held out both her hands to him in greeting. He took each of her hands in his own, bent his head, and placed a kiss on each of them.

"Mrs. Stern!"

"No! The name is Helen...Helen... Helen," she trilled.

"Then you must remember to call me 'Cal'."

He handed her the bouquet of red roses he had brought, and she placed them in a vase, which she half-filled with water. She brought out a thin bottle of white wine—actually the color was salmon-pink—and then poured some into a thin wine glass, which she handed to him, and poured a glass for herself. The glass was exquisite—tall, thin, a flower stalk and crystalline.

Cal held the glass up and turned it round a hundred and eighty degrees, and then back. The light was refracted through the glass as well as the wine, and he suddenly understood what Galileo, an Italian wine aficionado of the sixteenth century, as well as an astronomer, meant, when he described wine as 'liquid light'. They held up their glasses.

"To your Emeric," he said.

"To your Ruth," she responded.

Helen brought out a demitasse of espresso together with some delicacies, and they sat quietly and talked, with long pauses for reflection. During one of these pauses he noticed the oriental rugs that covered the floors and the ancient wall hangings, and a nostalgic memory of his first visit to the Sterns was revived.

She told him: "I read of Ruth's passing nearly two years ago. We wanted to visit you, but Emeric was already quite sick with cancer, and we could not go out."

"I'm glad you didn't," Calman replied, "or you would have found me wallowing in grief. I would not have been good company."

She said wistfully, "Ruth was a beautiful girl and very intelligent, and we loved her. It is too bad she had to die so young."

"Do you remember the broach you pinned on her lapel that first evening in this very apartment? Well she kept it to the very end. Now our daughter wears it."

"Oh! Calman, I would so much like to see your dear Elizabeth. She must miss her mother very much."

"Very much!" he muttered.

"And your Emeric was always a gentleman. I hope he did not suffer long."

There followed another time out for reflection, and then Calman broke in: "I should like to ask you something." She looked at him, waiting.

He took in a deep breath:

"When I first met you and your husband, thirty years ago, you were both fairly young, that is compared to our present ages."

"Yes," she replied, "We came to Canada in 1950. Emeric was fifty-one and I was fifty. And you, Cal, I don't think you were thirty."

"I was twenty-nine," he said, "and ready to conquer Mount Everest."

She smiled at the hyperbole. "You wanted to ask me something," she said.

He again took in a deep breath: "From the time we first met I was aware of a big difference between Emeric and yourself, not only in your deportments but in your dispositions. Emeric was stooped, and I thought I detected a limp when he walked. He was also usually preoccupied, turned towards his inner self. At the same time I found him to be a man of charm and elegance. You, on the other hand, bore yourself like a queen, upright and with authority, even though you always deferred to your husband, at least in public."

Helen explained, "Before the First World War, Emeric and I were engaged, and we intended to get married when he turned twenty. We were sweethearts, and we were in love. I never knew any other man. In 1917 he was conscripted and sent to the front, where he was forced to spend days lying in the filthy, wet trenches and to charge the enemy with open bayonets. He was wounded twice—once in the leg, which left him with a limp, and the second time he was gassed accidentally by his own officers."

A quiet ensued after Helena's words. Calman thought, *I should be leaving soon.* Speaking in a low voice he said sorrowfully: "I did not know." Unsteadied by this news he now made an awful gaffe. "Why did you not have any children?" He caught himself up: "*Damn! What's the matter with me? Now I've stepped over the line. How could I get so familiar? She'll think I'm an ill-bred oaf.*"

However, she didn't seem to mind his prying. In fact, she appeared to welcome the chance to confide a long held secret. "Because we were unable to have children," she said casually. You see, during the First World War, Emeric disappeared for a long time. We heard from him once to inform us he had been wounded, and to release me from my marriage vow. But I still waited for him, though several boys wanted to court me. Finally, when we did not hear from him again, believing he was dead, I did become engaged to a boy from my school days, Eric Berinsky. When Emeric finally did return I broke off with Eric, who was bitterly disappointed."

She smiled as she observed, "But he could not have been too disappointed because he was married within less than a year." She continued, "Emeric returned from the war damaged physically and mentally. At first he refused to see me. He remained in his room, and his only visitor was the doctor and the nurse who was hired to look after him. Eventually, when the weather improved, he would go for a stroll with his brother or sister. Sometimes Gula would join him. After a while he would go out by himself for long walks, and it was on such an outing that I ran into him. I hardly recognized him. He was thin and wasted and bent, and I felt more pity than love. He would not let me ask him questions about his war experiences, and later, when we parted and I asked him if he would like to go walking with me again he shrugged his shoulders and was non-committal.

"On one weekend I came to the house on the pretext of visiting Lily, and Emeric was home. He smiled at me, and I knew he was pleased to see me. Later, his mother told me that that was the first time he had smiled since arriving home. We took many walks after that. One day, as we were walking in a main shopping district we encountered a man dressed in checkered trousers and jacket and wearing a bowler hat. His shoes were three sizes too long, and he had red curly hair, which was a wig, of course, and his nose was painted red. He was selling roses. Emeric stopped to buy me a rose, and as we left the clown we enjoyed a hearty laugh. Later, we stopped off at a coffee shop and ordered apple strudel. He began to open up to me, and told me of his plans to join his father in the jewelry business. He had begun to sound like the Emeric of old.

"That evening I told my parents of the change in Emeric, and it was not long before they broached the subject of nuptials to the Sterns. They were delighted, but Emeric himself did not speak of marriage. One Saturday afternoon we took an exceptionally long walk, and it was I who raised the subject of marriage. 'Emeric,' I said, 'You have spoken of your future plans, and I am very pleased that you have settled on a vocation. But it seems to me that I am not included in these plans. We have spent a lot of time together now, and you have shown a lot of affection for me, but you have not kissed me, nor told me that you love me, as you once did.'

"He did not reply, but instead led me to a nearby park, and we sat down on a bench. Then, with a tremor in his voice he told me the reason. "You, Helena, are not only my beloved, but you are also my dearest friend. I have been trying to find a way to tell you something that I have kept secret from my family, and you have now opened a way for me to discuss it at least with you. During the war I was shot, not only in the foot, but also in the groin. After the doctors operated on me I was left impotent. I have been seeing doctors here about my condition, but they can do nothing about it. If I were to marry you I could never satisfy you. We could never have children. Our marriage would be empty.""

"We sat on that bench for a long time. I asked him, 'But Emeric, do you love me?'

"And he replied, 'With all my heart. I have never stopped loving you.'

"I told him: 'My life will be incomplete without you. We will find a way to cope.' And so we were married."

In the long quiet that followed, Calman, immersed in thought, soliloquized: "My God, this lovely, attractive, sensuous woman has gone through life without tasting the fruits of love, married yet unmarried, a flower that has never opened to the sunlight."

He saw the dewdrop tears moisten her eyes, and he enfolded her in his arms. She wept quietly, heaving gently against him. She wept for her lost years, for her lost Emeric, for those who were lost in the two wars. And he wept too for his own lost love. After a while, when both were calmed, he kissed her forehead and both of her cheeks, and she remained in his embrace. His fingers lingered over her breast, and he felt the quiver pass through her body. Then he bent and kissed the virgin lips, and she responded, and for the first time in two years he felt a stirring in his loins. She lifted her hand to his cheek and caressed it tenderly with the tips of her fingers, and she said to him:

"You know, Cal, I am an old woman."

He answered, "No. You are a beautiful woman."

But the momentary magic was gone, and Calman Mencher knew it was time to go and that they would not meet again.

Helena accompanied Calman to the door. There was no need to speak. He took her proffered hand and kissed it, and left. She closed the door, but in a moment opened it again.

"Calman," she called after him.

He was at the elevator, and turned back. "Calman," she said, "I almost forgot. There was something that Emeric wanted you to have." And she handed him the ebony cane.